JUST A KISS

A STANDALONE NOVELLA

J.H. CROIX

PREFACE

An earlier version of Just A Kiss was previously included in The Kristen Proby With Me in Seattle Universe. It was available in Kindle Unlimited for a limited time and has been out of publication since Dec 31, 2021. This is an updated version with all references to The Kristen Proby With Me in Seattle Universe removed and some other minor changes to the work. For additional clarification, J.H. Croix has always owned the full copyright to the work, however The Kristen Proby With Me in Seattle Universe had the rights for publication only for a period of time. Publication rights fully reverted to J.H. Croix, effective Dec 31, 2021.

Chapter One

JESSICA

When I climbed out of the car, my date, Chad, winked and flashed a quick smile as he reached for my hand. "I promise you'll like this."

Chad and I had been matched through a dating app. I'd been hesitant to dip my toes in the waters of dating, but my friend Daisy thought it was time for me to try dating someone. I kind of hated dating even though I did want to have a chance at a relationship with someone.

Chad seemed nice. He was a mid-level marketing executive at some tech company, but that was all I knew. We were supposed to keep our details private until we went on a second date.

While I didn't know much about him, I knew he was a sports fan as he'd promised me excellent seats for Seattle's current hot soccer team. Or, football, as he'd corrected me. While we walked toward the stadium, anticipation chased over my skin. I was a mostly casual sports fan, but I loved a live game.

Five minutes later, I was irritated. Chad somehow knew I was close friends with Daisy who happened to be married to Tristan Wells, one of the star players for the team. I could overlook him being nosy about me, but he'd clearly chosen this event for our date to try to get an "in" with the team for marketing connections. It was all I could do not to give him a swift kick in the shins and leave.

When Chad's hand came to rest on my lower back, annoyance flashed through me and not the good kind. "This way," he murmured, bending to place his mouth at my ear.

Apparently, Chad fancied himself a dominant kind of guy when he attempted to coax me into the team's private box for family and friends. I didn't think my personality would suit him. I suppose that was what I got for testing a new dating app.

Stopping abruptly, I swatted his hand away. "Chad, I'm not pushing my way in there."

His smile was so fake, my own face felt like it was about to crack. "Come on, Jessica, I know you have connections. It won't hurt anyone for you to make a few introductions for me."

Anger flared inside. "That's not the point. I met you less than an hour ago. I'm not some kind of connection for you to leverage. I'm done with this date."

Turning to walk away, I seriously considered marching into the box just to tell Daisy what a disaster this date was. She'd cajoled me into it, telling me to at least give dating a chance. She'd even reviewed Chad's bullshit bio and pointed out most of the bios weren't too useful, so I might as well try.

"Jessica," a voice said, the tone commanding and low.

The sound of my name sent a wash of goose bumps over my skin. As if caught by a silk lasso, my feet came to an abrupt stop, and I turned toward the voice.

I knew it wasn't Chad. He didn't sound like that. I scanned the area with people milling ahead of the game before my eyes collided with an icy-blue gaze. My breath felt locked in my lungs, and my pulse shot into the stratosphere. Hayes Maddox stood ten feet away, exuding calm power and understated masculinity. Hayes was the kind of man women ruined panties over, and he didn't even have to try. It was there in the lift of his chiseled chin, the stark lines of his cheekbones, and the intense look in his eyes.

Heat suffused me, spinning like fire throughout my entire body. I'd been an intern at Hayes's tech firm in Seattle three years ago. I'd had a terrible crush on him, like the worst kind, but I was certain he'd never noticed me. Though I also would've argued he didn't even know my name.

Apparently, I was wrong on that count.

"She's with me." Chad's voice came from over my shoulder.

"No, I'm not. Not anymore," I said, my anger snapping me out of my shock.

Hayes approached in a deceptively lazy stride as he ignored everyone around us. His intent eyes locked on Chad. "That's not what she says."

Oh, God. Hayes's voice was just as sexy as I remembered. It was low with a thread of command and the expectation that anyone he spoke to was listening.

My nipples sure were. They tightened up the second he took another step to stand closer to me.

Chad's eyes bounced to me. "Jessica,

would you please clarify that we came here tonight together?”

Oh, for God's sake. I was not going to shore up Chad's stupid ego.

“We may have arrived together, but I'm no longer your date. I just said so not two minutes ago. Now, if you'll excuse me.”

I started to walk away only to have dumbass Chad try to follow. This time, Hayes cut right in front of him. “I think she's made it clear she's not with you.”

Chad muttered something and stalked away, actually pouting. I was caught between my annoyance with Chad and this decidedly inconvenient effect Hayes was having on me.

“Would you like a ride home?” Hayes asked. It sounded more like an order than a question.

So I said as much. “Is that really a question, Hayes? Also, the game hasn't even started.” I was a little surprised at my boldness. I'd used his name to make it clear that I knew who he was.

His lips quirked at the corners as he shrugged. “It hasn't, but it doesn't matter.”

Next thing I knew, Hayes had rested his palm between my shoulder blades and was coaxing me forward. For the life of me, I couldn't think of one reason not to leave, but it got my spine up to have him being the one to insist I do so.

But this *was* Hayes, and he'd once intimidated me just by existing. Plus, he did kind of make my knees melt.

Moments later, I found myself out on the sidewalk. "Did you drive here yourself?" he asked, his blue eyes boring into me.

I wanted to lie, I really did. But I couldn't summon myself to do that under the force of a presence like Hayes's. "No."

Hayes didn't even reply. He gestured for me to walk ahead of him, his hand landing at the dip of my waist like a hot brand. We crossed the street while he made a quick phone call. After a few words, he slid his phone in his pocket.

"I can find my way home. I'll just call a car service."

Hayes looked at me quietly, and I shut up. "My car is here."

In another moment, he was holding open the back door of a sleek black sedan. God, this was crazy.

Hayes climbed in beside me and closed the door. "Your address?" he asked.

I quickly recited it, and he repeated it to the driver. "If you don't mind, some privacy please, Danny," he added.

"You got it, boss."

A partition rolled up with a whisper between the front and the back. I laced my fingers together and clasped them over my knees. I was even dressed up because Daisy told me I needed to look good for a date. My skirt was bright blue and twirly around my knees, and I'd paired it with these cute little kitten heels.

"I'm glad you left," Hayes began.

"I'm surprised you even know my name," I countered.

One of Hayes's dark brows rose in a slash. "You think I would forget your name?"

HAYES

Jessica Slater crossed and uncrossed her legs as she stared at me. The space inside the car felt crowded with nothing but a narrow strip of the black leather seat between us. Seeing Jessica tonight had surprised me.

I was downright furious with the asshole who'd been trying to cajole her into the private team box, but that was a problem for another day.

Jessica lifted a hand, smoothing it over her dark locks. The streetlights outside flickered through the window, glinting on her hair. She finally lifted a shoulder in a small shrug. "I'm still surprised you remember my name," she said in her husky voice.

"I have a good memory," I countered.

Jessica traced her finger along the stitching on the seat between us, and I wished she was tracing her finger anywhere on me. Jessica had been an intern at my company some years ago. She'd been totally off-limits. Interns weren't a part of my social circle. Especially not interns who affected me like a live wire of electricity to my system. Somehow, she was even sexier now.

"I don't think you ever spoke my name when I was working at your company. Why would I assume you would ever remember it?"

Oh, that's right. Jessica was assertive. Or so her boss had told me. Well, I suppose I'd been her boss as well, but I didn't directly manage the interns at my company.

Since leaving her internship, she'd gone on to start her own gaming company. It was small but well-known. She made it a point to work with determined, like-minded women and had made a splash with several successful games. She was brilliant, and I wouldn't mind stealing her back.

"Maybe we didn't talk much, but I remember you. Obviously."

Jessica pursed her lips. She was wearing a

shiny lip gloss I wanted to kiss off, but no other makeup that I could tell. I quickly did the math in my head. She'd been an intern about four years ago, which meant she was twenty-three years old, or thereabouts, when she was at my company. It would've been right after she graduated from an advanced master's program in computer coding.

I sponsored that program and hosted ten interns a year. Not only was it an excellent program but it was also a way to scope out the best talent. My tech company had started in gaming, but we had expanded into secure social and dating apps and security services for a variety of social media applications.

So that made Jessica about twenty-seven years old now, only five years younger than me. It was perfectly acceptable for me to pursue her now.

"So you do," she finally said, flicking her hair off her shoulder.

When her big, dark eyes met mine, it felt as if a little bolt of lightning sizzled through the air between us. She had a standoffish vibe, one that made me want to break down her barriers.

"Do you intend to go on a second date with your friend there?" I asked.

Jessica let out a little huff, her nostrils flaring as she looked at me. "Absolutely not."

"Good. He's an asshole," I said flatly.

She snorted. "How do you know?"

"Because he was after connections only."

Jessica twisted her mouth to the side. "Serves me right. I didn't want to try a dating app, but my friend convinced me."

"Which app?"

"Metro Love."

The moment she said the name of the app, annoyance flashed inside. Because my company was involved in the app's development. "Well, then. I'll make sure he's kicked off that app."

Jessica gave me a quizzical look, furrowing her brows. "Oh," she said as her expression cleared. "Your company must be an investor. No need to kick him off just because of me. I don't intend to use it again."

"No?"

She shook her head, her hair shifting lightly on her shoulders. "It wasn't really for me to begin with."

I had thoughts, lots of them, namely wanting to tell Jessica not to bother with *any* dating app. I might have put her out of my mind, but seeing her now set me on fire, and I wanted her.

"They're not for everybody," I replied, trying to keep my tone casual.

We turned onto the street where she lived. "It's right there," she said, gesturing to a small bungalow house, a style of home popular in the Northwest.

My driver stopped, and I tapped on the window for him to roll down the partition. "I'll walk from here, Danny."

"Got it. See you tomorrow," he replied with a nod.

"Thank you," Jessica called.

A moment later, we were on the sidewalk, and the car was rolling away. Jessica looked up at me. "You can't live close to here. I don't think this neighborhood is nice enough for you."

Looking down at her, I felt my lips curl in a smile. "It so happens I only live a few blocks away. I grew up in Seattle, so I prefer neighborhoods like this."

Jessica's eyes widened slightly. "Well, the king climbs down from his throne."

She was so sassy. Because I had avoided her when she was an intern, I'd never seen this side of her. "I'm not a king."

"Maybe not. You just have piles of money and run one of the hottest tech companies in Seattle," she returned.

"Don't try to convince me you're not doing well. Your company may be small, but you've had two major hits. Now, let me walk you to your door, please."

"What if I said no?"

"I would wait here until you went inside."

Jessica eyed me for another few beats before she turned and walked up the slate pathway that led to the porch. Since she didn't chase me off, I followed.

We stopped in front of her door, and I looked down. Once again, the second my eyes snagged on hers, it felt as if lightning sizzled, and the hairs on the back of my neck prickled.

This girl. Damn. She got to me.

"I'd like to see you again."

Jessica had been reaching for her keys in her purse and went still. Her eyes swung up to mine again, and she parted her lips in surprise. "Excuse me?"

"I'd like to see you again," I repeated.

When she stayed silent, I prompted, "Tell me when."

I heard the swift intake of her breath through her lips, and desire jolted through me. I waited.

"Um," she finally began, "somehow, I don't think I'm your type."

"That's where you're wrong."

I'd been keeping a safe distance between us so I didn't do anything stupid. But now I had a point to prove.

In two strides, I was standing right in front of her. She opened her mouth to speak, but I lifted my finger and placed it over her lips. "Let me show you something," I murmured.

Dropping my hand, I eased close enough that when she took in a gulp of air, I could feel her breasts rise and brush against my chest through the thin silk of her blouse. When I lifted my hand to slide it around and cup the back of her neck, her hair was just as silky as I imagined. She took in another breath, and I dipped my head, silently telling myself to keep this quick and not let it spiral out of control.

I waited just long enough for her to step back if she really didn't want this. But she *did* want it. I knew she did. The chemistry between us was creating its own electrical storm.

Her dark eyes held mine. I dipped my head and brushed my lips over hers—once, twice, and then, her lashes swept against her cheeks and her eyes closed. Tangling my fingers in her hair, I finally fit my mouth over hers, telling myself I could have just a little bit more. She smelled like flowers, and her mouth tasted sweet. She let out a little sigh, followed by a whimper that caught at the back of her throat.

When her tongue darted out to glide against mine, I groaned into her mouth, diving into her warm sweetness and taking our kiss deeper. I lost my mind when she arched against me and let out a breathy moan. My hands slid through her silky locks and down her spine to cup her bottom and pull her against me. She gasped.

The sound of a car door slamming on the street filtered through the fuzz of lust in my mind. I scrambled for control and tore my mouth away, pressing hot open-mouthed kisses along her jaw before dipping my head and breathing her in.

This was plain crazy. I was kissing her senseless on her porch. Maybe I could talk myself into thinking it was sensible because I'd known her before, but it wasn't. Not really.

I did *not* want to leave, but I would. Grasping onto my control, I slowly lifted my head and stepped back reluctantly. Jessica stared at me, her cheeks pink under the soft light cast from above her door. Her lips were swollen, and I wanted to see her undone.

"Dinner next Friday."

"Okay," she whispered.

Chapter Three

JESSICA

"He what?" Sarah asked, her eyes wide.

"He was an asshole. I don't know how, but he knew I was friends with people who know the team, and he wanted to be introduced. It pissed me off."

Sarah popped the lid on her coffee and reached for another packet of sugar. As she tore it open and added it to her coffee, she replied, "Wow. I wanted you to get out of your comfort zone, but not with a jerk."

I leaned back in my desk chair, spinning to check my email on my laptop when I heard the distinct ping sound. It was nothing I needed to deal with at the moment, so I closed my computer and spun back to face Sarah. "I wouldn't have liked him even if he hadn't done that. He was too cocky for me. You're not gonna believe this, though."

She took a swallow of her coffee before lowering it and eyeing me. "What?"

"I ran into Hayes Maddox there. He insisted on giving me a ride home."

She'd just taken another sip of her coffee and sputtered before setting it down and reaching for a tissue from the box on the corner of my desk. "You are freaking kidding me."

Sarah had also been an intern at Hayes's company. Our journey as friends had started as roommates in college. We became besties through our shared love of gaming, and we were blessed to be able to work together. Sarah had zero interest (her words) in running a company, so she had chosen to come work with me even though she had other offers. Our working relationship was made even better because I trusted her completely, and she didn't mind disagreeing with me.

"Not kidding." My cheeks flushed. "He also invited me to dinner."

I couldn't bring myself to tell her about the kiss. Somehow, it felt too private. I didn't feel right gossiping about how insanely hot and intimate it had been. That happened on Friday night. It was now Monday morning, and I must've replayed that kiss a hundred times in my mind. Mathematically, it couldn't have lasted more than sixty seconds, yet it was burned into me.

"You said yes, right? You'd better have agreed to dinner with him," Sarah demanded.

"Of course, I did." The moment I spoke, all my insecurities started clamoring inside. "I don't know what I was thinking, though. Hayes is *way* out of my league."

"He is *not* out of your league. You run a company too. You won an award just this year for women's entrepreneurship in Seattle. You're a fucking badass," Sarah said, being the good friend she was.

I drummed my fingertips on my desk. "I don't know. I'll see if I have the nerve to go to dinner with him by the time Friday rolls around. Funny side note: he's an investor in that dating app. He was none too happy to see Chad being a jerk."

"Forget Chad. I think it was meant to be," Sarah said, her blue eyes wide. "I mean, you ran into Hayes there, and now, you're having dinner with him." She held her palm over her chest as she spoke in a breathy voice.

Sarah was a total romantic. She'd been casting her net far and wide to find her forever after. Lately, she'd been trying to rope me into her project because I hadn't gone on a date in three years. It was for a good reason. I'd been busy building my business.

"Oh, for crying out loud. It wasn't meant to be. Hayes just happened to be there, and I just happened to dump my date right in front of him."

Sarah cocked her head to the side, her blue eyes twinkling. She was the kind of pretty that would be annoying if she wasn't so freaking awesome. She was truly the blond-haired, blue-eyed kind of cute I used to avoid. As friends, that was. We ended up paired together for a research project in a coding class and then became roommates. Behind her beauty, I discovered the heart of a brilliant brain and a bubbly soul. I adored her.

She wrinkled her nose. "But he asked you out to dinner, didn't he?" she teased in a sing-song voice.

My cheeks were getting hotter by the second. Needing a distraction, I rolled my eyes and flipped my laptop open again. "We'll see if I go. Meanwhile, I need to work. We've got a slew of applications to go through. You're going to sit with me for the interviews, right?" We were interviewing for a new assistant position for one of our projects.

Sarah stood from the chair where she was sitting on the other side of my desk, smoothing her hands down her jeans. "In case I need to remind you, you're my boss. If you want me to sit in on the interviews, then I'll be there. I'd like to because we're both going to be working on this project."

Every now and then, I forgot I was actually her boss. I'd started this company by myself after I made a single game that took off by chance. A simple word scramble game that was "crazy addictive with a waterfall flow of words on the screen." Or at least, that was how the online gaming site review described it. The steady sales from that game had given me the capital to expand and make more gaming apps.

"Right," I said with a nod. "Yes, I'd like you to sit in on them. I'll send over a batch of these resumes, and we can sort through them together."

Sarah started to walk out with her coffee in hand. "Don't forget your lid," I added, pointing at where she'd left her coffee lid on my desk when she was cleaning up her sputter, along with a piece of tissue. She snatched them up quickly and turned away again. Stopping in my doorway, she gave me a sly smile. "Don't you dare cancel the dinner date with Hayes. If you do, I'll make you regret it."

Rolling my eyes, I waved her out of my office. The second she was gone, the memory of Hayes's lips on mine burned like a flare in my thoughts.

Chapter Four

HAYES

"I want him deleted," I said flatly.

My assistant, Brian, looked at me from over the top of his glasses. "I think that's a bit much. If you interfere like that, we're going to get questions about it. What am I supposed to say?" Brian glanced down and brushed an invisible crumb off his shoulder.

Brian was gorgeous and often had women drooling over him. Too bad for them because he was happily married to his high school boyfriend. I paid him good money to stay on as my assistant because he was one of the few people who didn't mind questioning me. I needed that.

"Do tell me why you're asking for this guy

to be deleted," Brian added with a pointed and knowing look. Brian was also one of the few people who could pry the truth out of me.

"I was at the game the other night—" I began.

Brian immediately cut in, "Another night out?"

"Yes. Do you have a problem with that?"

"Not a problem but an observation. You're bored and you're afraid of a relationship."

Putting my hand on my chest, I let out a mock sigh. "Wow. That's kind of harsh."

"And precisely accurate," he returned swiftly.

Dropping my hand, I drummed my fingertips on the glass surface of my desk. "Can I finish explaining?"

"Please do," he said, circling his hand in the air.

"So, I ran into Jessica Slater. Do you recall her?"

"Yes. She was an intern here, and you did your damnedest to ignore just how cute she is. She started that company that took off. I'd say her coding days here paid off. She's on the potential companies list I drew up for you to partner with for new ventures. Everybody loves her. She was born and raised in Seattle, her dad was a fisherman, and her mom grew up on a farm nearby. She's got a great backstory, and she's committed to all things Seattle. She just won some women's business award."

"She did?"

Brian nodded, a glint in his eyes. "Wow. I knew something you didn't. But I wouldn't expect you to pay attention to women's entrepreneurship awards. You're not eligible by virtue of your gender."

"I care about women doing well in business. I have equal pay policies voluntarily, I might add."

Brian smirked. "I know you like credit for everything, but I happen to be one of those people who doesn't think we should get a pat on the back for doing the decent thing."

I chuckled. "Fair enough. Anyway, back to the other night. Jessica was there. The asshole I want deleted brought her there on a first date and tried to bully her into introducing him to her friends who she knows on the team. She met him through that app. We have a policy against that kind of pushy behavior on the app."

"Did you come to her rescue?" he teased.

"It wasn't necessary. She dumped him right in front of me, which is how I knew what happened. I did give her a ride home."

"Aaaa-nd?"

"I invited her to dinner Friday."

"Did she say yes?"

"Reluctantly," I admitted.

Brian threw his head back with a laugh. When he sobered, he leveled his gaze with mine again. "Good. You need someone who's not going to just fall at your feet. Jessica doesn't need you for anything, not even your connections."

"I know," I grumbled, annoyed with myself for being annoyed.

"You're seriously interested in her," Brian observed.

When I met his gaze, I almost winced. Brian knew me too well—sometimes better than I knew myself. "I guess I am."

Brian gave me an assessing look. "Are you going to try to be real about her? Or jut string her along? Jessica doesn't strike me as someone who wants to waste time."

I contemplated his observation about me and relationships, or lack thereof. My mind spun to how possessive I felt about Jessica. She made me want more.

Brian's phone vibrated, and he slipped it out of his shirt pocket to glance at the screen. "I need to take this. It's Harold from accounting." He stood from his chair and eyed me. "You'd better treat Jessica well. Or I'll personally kick your ass."

Chapter Five

JESSICA

"I don't even have his phone number," I muttered.

Winston, my slender orange swirl cat, blinked his round blue eyes at me, offering no comment on this.

How was I supposed to text Hayes a lame excuse when I didn't have his number?

Maybe I wasn't supposed to chicken out. If I let myself think, which I did *all* the freaking time, I knew it was because that kiss intimidated me. His money, or his stature, or how crazy sexy and handsome he was didn't bother me. No, it was just a kiss that lasted for less than sixty seconds of my time.

The whole time I had my stupid crush on him when I was an intern, I'd told myself he could never live up to the hype in my mind. Now, Hayes had gone and given me a masterful, panty-melting, knee-weakening, turn-a-girl-into-a-needy-bundle kind of kiss.

I couldn't imagine that kiss was as mind-blowing for him as it was for me. I mean, my God, he was probably accustomed to women who had far more experience than I did. I simply didn't make time for romance or dating. During college, my focus had been on graduating at the top of my class. The same went for my master's program. That didn't leave much time for dating. I'd only had two actual boyfriends—one in high school and one in college—and then a scorching, hot as hell single kiss with Hayes.

I stroked my hand over Winston's back, and he emitted an appreciative purr. My mind started doing laps again on how to reach Hayes and cancel our dinner date. I supposed I could call his office. It was late, approaching midnight actually, and I was still working. Knowing that I couldn't solve this small problem tonight, I slipped my laptop closer to me on the couch and tapped on the screen, surprised to see a new email appear with a friendly ping.

The email came from onehotkissonyourporch at maddox dot com.

The second I saw his last name, my pulse skyrocketed, and I felt hot all over. *Jesus*. It was near midnight, and I was sitting alone on the couch with my freaking cat. I took a deep breath.

Calm the fuck down. I talked to myself sometimes, more than I preferred. I took a deep breath and tapped to open his email.

Hayes: *I have your phone number, but I didn't want to be rude and use it without confirming it was okay with you. I'd like to pick you up at 7pm on Friday. How does Thai food sound?*

This was followed by his official email signature.

And then, *p.s. I can't wait to taste you again.*

I felt a throb between my thighs at his comment. He wanted to taste me?

My hands trembled as they hovered over the keyboard. I told myself I should tell him I couldn't go to dinner.

Instead, I typed, *I love Thai food. 7 sounds great.*

My finger hit send before I could make it stop. The moment I heard that little whooshing sound, like a cartoon plane taking off, I muttered, "Oh, my God. I'm such an idiot."

Within seconds, my email pinged again. My head whipped up to see his reply already waiting in my inbox. Practically frantic, I tapped the button to open it.

Hayes: *Did you miss the last part of my email?*

How the hell was I supposed to reply to that?

Jessica: *Of course not. That kiss was nice.*

Oh, my God. I'd just described his kiss as nice.

Nice? was his only reply.

Pushing to my feet abruptly, I paced in a tiny circle in my living room.

That kiss was so much more than nice, but I wasn't used to this kind of dialogue. After several breathing attempts, I sat down and decided just to be honest.

Jessica: *It was way more than nice.*

My shaky hands hit the send key. Winston eyed me quizzically. I didn't blame him for being confused because I was acting like an idiot. I was usually confident, yet between my disaster of a first date and then Hayes's kiss, I felt unsettled in a way I hadn't before.

I prided myself on feeling confident. It's just my confidence extended solely to my professional life. I was relieved Sarah didn't happen to be here. She would know me well enough to make an observation about my antsy state of being.

"Winston, he's not replying," I said to my

cat, who merely eyed me curiously and licked his crotch.

I sat back down on the couch, letting my breath out in a gust. Idly stroking my knuckles under Winston's chin, I looked at him before moving to stroke his back. My relationship with my cat was far less complicated than trying to date. Especially trying to date a man like Hayes.

My laptop pinged again, and I practically pulled a muscle in my neck when I turned to look. Hayes's private email popped up again.

I reached over with my left hand and quickly tapped to open his email.

Hayes: *It was definitely way more than nice.*

My belly swooped, and heat raced over my skin.

Chapter Six

HAYES

It was almost midnight. I was sitting on my couch with my cat, Winston, perched on my knees. Winston, an ancient smoky gray cat I'd inherited from my grandmother when she passed away, looked at me curiously.

"For a cat who's almost blind, you sure look like you have an opinion," I observed as I stared back at him.

Winston blinked his foggy eyes and began purring. He did that, just purred out of nowhere, all the time. He dipped his head down and rubbed his ear against my thigh as I looked back at my laptop screen.

That was how bad I had it for Jessica. I created an entirely secure, private email at my office so that I could email her. I was sitting here like a teenage boy waiting for a girl to return a text. I did have her number. I'd actually gotten it by digging through HR's online files from when she did her internship.

Yet I hadn't felt quite right about texting her directly, so I'd resorted to this.

Several long minutes passed after my last email where I had mostly parroted what she said. She finally replied.

Jessica: *Define nice.*

I felt my lips tugging into a smile. I tapped the email open and began typing my reply.

Hayes: *Nice is coffee that's a little weak but decent. Nice is something that meets my expectations and doesn't bother me. Nice is a reliable car that I'm not in love with.*

Perhaps it would be better if I tell you what's not nice. Because nice isn't memorable, not usually. Nice doesn't sear itself into your memory. Nice is not a kiss that sets you on fire.

I tapped the send button. When I leaned back into the couch cushions, I became aware of the rapid pounding of my heart and the way my entire body was tight. My balls were tightening, and my cock was swelling.

All over an email exchange.

Yet again, the time between my email and hers felt long. But the distinctive chime eventually came, and I saw the banner with her email address.

With Winston still purring away beside me, I tapped to open it.

Jessica: *On fire?*

Although I could've interpreted what Jessica was doing as calculated teasing, I knew better. That just wasn't her personality at all. She was remarkably straightforward. Although I had limited my interactions with her when she was an intern—as Brian had pointed out, I totally had the hots for her—I paid close attention during any communications. I had also followed her, as I did anyone who worked for us after they left, and she was well-known in the business world for being straightforward and honest. Because she was a woman, some people took that as aggressive. Women just couldn't win sometimes.

I typed my reply. *Yes, kissing you set me on fire. Way more than nice. Can I see you before Friday?*

Jessica: *Friday is tomorrow.*

There she went being straightforward. I chuckled.

Hayes: *So it is. Forgive me for losing track. I'll see you at seven.*

Jessica: *Does it matter what I wear? I'm not sure what restaurant we're going to.*

The feel of Jessica's bottom under my palm and that silky and twirly skirt she'd been wearing the other night came to mind. My cock swelled to an ache.

Hayes: *No. Wear whatever you'd like.*

I congratulated myself on my restraint.

Jessica: *But is it a fancy restaurant?*

Hayes: *It's Thai food. It's not that fancy. I want you to be yourself.*

Jessica: *Okay. Good night, Hayes.*

Hayes: *Good night, Jessica.*

Chapter Seven

JESSICA

Smoothing my hands over my gauzy skirt, I looked myself over with a critical eye. I was wearing a comfortable skirt because I was nervous, but Daisy assured me it was cute. I had actually just texted her a photo of my outfit. She couldn't come over and help me get dressed tonight because she had a late night at work.

My skirt was royal blue, and it was spring in Seattle, so I could expect it to get chilly this evening. I was wearing a pair of fitted black boots. A cream-colored camisole with a matching silk blouse over it topped off my look. I wrinkled my nose when eyeing my dark hair. It was thin and didn't hold a curl no matter what I did. The streaks of burgundy

I'd whimsically added here and there added a hint of fun though. As I stared at myself in the mirror, I contemplated whether I should try some eye makeup. I decided against it, if only because I was afraid I would screw it up.

With a swipe of lip gloss on my lips, I decided I had to be ready. I didn't have time to think further because the doorbell rang.

"Shit, shit, shit," I muttered as I grabbed my jacket, a lightweight number that belted around my waist, and hurried into the living room.

My pulse was racing, and I forced myself to stop and take a breath. I didn't need to answer the door all breathless. As I took another breath, I felt Winston staring at me. I almost said something, but I worried Hayes might be able to hear me through the door. He didn't need to know I was a crazy person who talked to my cat.

Crossing the room, I swung the door open. The moment I did, my breath caught in my throat and my belly did a tickly flip. Hayes looked good enough to eat.

The setting sun glinted on his dark hair, and his blue eyes were bright when they met mine. He was wearing jeans that fit his muscled legs like a lover. Atop that, he wore a fitted Henley shirt that did nothing to disguise his build. I couldn't imagine Hayes working out at a gym, but clearly, the guy did something to stay in shape.

I didn't realize I hadn't spoken yet until Hayes said, "Hey."

I swallowed and tried to take a breath, although my lungs were struggling at their one and only job. My "Hey" came out squeaky. "Are you early?"

Hayes's lips twitched, his eyes still on me. "Maybe a few minutes. Are you ready?"

I was about to say yes when I realized I didn't have my purse. "Just about. Come on in. I need to get my purse."

He stepped in and shut the door behind him, waiting right there as I hurried back into my bedroom to snatch my purse off my dresser. When I returned to the living room, Winston was winding around Hayes's calves, and Hayes leaned over to pet him.

"What's your cat's name?" he asked as he scratched between Winston's ears.

"Winston."

Hayes straightened quickly. "You're kidding."

"Uh, no. That's his name."

Winston continued his tight loops around Hayes's legs. Hayes stared at me for a long moment. "That's weird. My cat's name is Winston too."

"You're kidding!"

"Definitely not. Although I didn't name him. I got him from my grandmother after she passed away."

My heart gave an achy beat. Oh, my God. Hayes had his grandmother's cat. That made him seem kind of sweet, and I didn't know what to think about him being hot *and* sweet.

"I'm glad you could take care of her cat, and I'm sorry to hear she passed away."

"Thank you." He inclined his head slightly. "She lived a good life, but I still miss her. I promised her I'd take care of Winston."

We stood there quietly for a moment, just staring at each other. It felt as if the air around us filled with hot sparks.

"Are you ready to go now?" Hayes finally asked.

Leaning back in my chair, I put my hand over my belly. "I think I ate too much."

Hayes's eyes lifted as he set his napkin down. "Same here." When his lips spread in a slow smile from one corner to the other, I felt my own automatically curling in return.

Hayes knew how to take a woman on a dinner date. As promised, he'd taken me to a delicious Thai restaurant. Then he insisted we come to this dessert café recently opened by a friend of his. I'd gotten vanilla flan with a raspberry glaze while Hayes had gone for a rich chocolate mousse.

The friend in question, Drew, stopped by our table. His brown eyes twinkled as he glanced back and forth between us. "How was it?" He lifted our empty plates and set them on the tray resting on his forearm.

"Absolutely amazing. That was some of the best flan I've ever had," I replied.

His eyes flicked to Hayes. "And you, my friend?"

"Amazing. You do dangerous things with chocolate."

Drew chuckled. "My goal is to do dangerous things with every dessert. I hope you two come back soon."

"Of course, we will," Hayes replied as Drew turned, casting me a quick wink before moving to check on another table.

"How in the world does he stay in shape and run a dessert café?" I mused.

Hayes shrugged. "Good question. I do know he's a marathon runner. That's how we met."

"You run marathons?" I didn't even try to hide my surprise.

Hayes shook his head, replying, "I ran *one* marathon. I don't have time for the training. Drew and I met running cross-country together in high school."

"Where did you go to high school?"

"Right here in Seattle. Rumor has it you did too."

"I did. I was born and raised here. But it seems you know that."

My cheeks flushed again, and my eyes dropped from Hayes's. He had no problem with sustained eye contact, but sometimes, it was more than I could handle.

My gaze was drawn downward to where he was folding a napkin into a shape. While I should've been curious about what he was doing, I got hung up on his hands instead. He had long, nimble fingers and strong hands. Everything about him screamed strong and masculine. I had a flash of memory—the feel of his palm sliding down my back and cupping my bottom last week. Immediately following that was the recollection of the hard, hot length of his arousal pressed against me when he kissed me.

I forced my eyes up, only to run right into

his gaze again. I had no idea how much time had passed, maybe a few seconds.

He picked up the thread of our conversation. "I did know you grew up here. Although it wasn't on your resume when you applied for your internship, your company has made a little splash, and you're Seattle's tech sweetheart since you're from the area."

I rolled my eyes. "I'm nobody's sweetheart."

Hayes watched me quietly. He didn't speak, but his eyes said all kinds of things. Butterflies took flight in my belly, and my pulse began humming along. My lack of experience with men was biting me in the ass. Who knew I could get all hot and bothered just from a look?

My eyes dropped again, landing on whatever he was doing with the napkin. "What are you making?"

When I mustered the courage to withstand the heat of his gaze, I looked up.

"A bird." He lifted the neatly folded napkin. "Here." He handed it across the table to me.

"I don't want to mess it up." He placed it lightly on my open palm. It looked like a tiny seagull.

"It's only meant to be temporary. It is a napkin, after all."

"Aside from running one marathon, is origami another one of your talents?"

Hayes held my eyes for a hot, liquid moment. "Maybe. It's something I do when I need to keep my hands occupied."

"You need something to do with your hands now?" I asked.

"Well, yes. I'm trying to be appropriate."

With his eyes like liquid fire on me, my breath hitched, and heat spun through me. Next thing I knew, he slid around the curved booth in the corner of the café until I felt his thigh flush against mine.

I was silent—not by calculation, but by sheer desire overload. Was that a thing? I supposed it was with Hayes.

When I dared a glance, I found his gaze waiting, that intense blue darkening as we looked at each other. I felt his palm slide on my thigh. Maybe I didn't want him to be appropriate.

Chapter Eight

HAYES

Jessica was fucking stunning. She was all the more intoxicating simply because she didn't try too hard. The lip gloss I'd wanted to kiss off had disappeared while she savored her food. She wore another skirt that I wanted to flip up so I could see what kind of panties she wore underneath. All evening, with her camisole tight across her breasts, I thought about teasing her nipples.

As hard as the spurs of need were driving me, I didn't want to rush. I didn't want to blow through her guard and ruin this. I heard the hitch of her breath in her throat and watched her lashes sweep against her cheeks when she dipped her head to look down at where my palm rested on her thigh. I could feel the heat of her skin through the gauzy fabric and wondered what her bare skin would feel like under my touch.

I'd been holding my need at bay for most of the evening, willing my arousal to cool whenever I had to stand so that I didn't embarrass myself. I was accustomed to being in control and distantly shocked at how little I had around Jessica.

I slid my hand down toward her knee and back up. When I felt the garter underneath her skirt, a hot shot of blood arrowed to my groin. *Not happening tonight*, I told myself. As desperately as I wanted Jessica, I was not going to take things all the way tonight. I sensed she had formed expectations about me, and I intended to prove them wrong.

"Jessica," I murmured, my voice a little tighter than I wished. My control was stretched, so I could only manage so much.

Those lashes swept up, and her big brown eyes met mine. Her eyes searched my face, and I wondered what she was looking for. Meanwhile, I slid my hand down her thigh again, this time catching the hem of her skirt.

Her tongue darted out, sliding from one corner of her bottom lip to the other. Her pupils were dilated, and I could see the rapid flutter of her pulse in her neck. I didn't realize I was moving closer until her sweet, tangy scent hit me like a fucking drug. I inhaled deeply as my lips met her skin, right where her pulse beat.

She sucked a breath in, and I forced myself to lift my head. It was a physical effort because my body was so reluctant to leave the taste of her. My fingers met her sheer stockings, and I slowly walked them up her thigh, feathering along the inside edge. All the while, her eyes held mine. I felt as if I was falling, diving into this bottomless pool of need and want, tangled up inside a puzzling wish to please her beyond just physically.

I paused when my first fingertip landed on her bare skin. "You can tell me to stop."

Her nostrils flared when she took another breath. "Okay." That one word came out breathy, and it was like the lash of a whip on the flanks of my need. I was already racing, the pace so fast I might stumble.

"Does okay mean you want me to stop?" I pressed because I needed to know.

She shook her head, just barely. I lifted my hand lightly and placed one finger at a time on the silky soft skin of the inside of her thigh. As if playing scales on the piano, I moved my touch up purposely. I paused right when I met the juncture where her thigh creased, almost growling out loud when I felt her skin pebble under my touch.

"What are you doing?" she whispered.

"I want to make you come."

So much for taking things slow.

Her pretty brown eyes widened, and her mouth parted slightly as she took in a gulp of air. "Here?"

She finally broke free of my gaze to look around the intimate café. The place was busy, the noise masking any conversation we were having. And Drew, because he was my friend, had given us a private booth tucked in a corner with nothing but a little light above us. If anyone were to look in our direction, they would see me beside her, talking in a low voice and nothing more. A tablecloth obscured anything my hands were doing underneath the table.

When her eyes made their way back to me, I said, "No one can see." My hand remained completely still. "I'll stop," I added when I saw a twitch of worry between her brows.

I began to move my hand away, but then she shook her head sharply. "Don't stop."

Well, then. There was nothing I loved more than permission. This time, I let my hand slide down to cup her mound. "Open your knees," I whispered in her ear.

I couldn't resist dropping a kiss just behind her ear and loved the way her body trembled. She parted her knees a little bit more, and I let my fingers slide down to press over the very heart of her. It was hot, and her panties were damp.

Although I didn't doubt she wanted this, I was acutely aware we were in a public place, and I couldn't let this drag out forever. I scraped that damp silk out of the way and didn't even bother to hide my groan when my fingers found her slick core. I dabbled for just a moment, teasing a little bit and loving the way her hips rocked into my touch and her breath came in sharp little pants.

Then I sank one finger inside her, not waiting to add another as she gasped, and her pussy rippled around my touch. I leaned down farther to press another kiss on the side of her neck as I began fucking her slowly with my fingers.

"Hayes." Her voice was frayed as her hips moved with the rhythm of my fingers.

"Yes, Jessica?"

She started to say something, but then

her release struck, and her entire body went taut before she shuddered. She began to make a sound, and I immediately fit my mouth over hers, catching her whimpers in our kiss.

Chapter Nine

JESSICA

My knees were liquid as Hayes escorted me out of the café. Somehow, my manners helped me to form words and politely thank Drew for the delicious dessert. I even managed to assure him I would be back.

I distantly wondered if he could tell I was practically drunk on pleasure. My body was still reverberating with the echoes of it. Hayes's hand rested between my shoulder blades as we walked through the door out onto the sidewalk. A light mist was falling, the cool drops striking my heated cheeks.

His hand slid down my back to curl around the edge of my hip. His touch felt both possessive and comforting. I wanted to lean into him. My eyes had just been opened shockingly wide when it came to sensual pleasure, and we hadn't even had sex. We were both fully dressed, and he'd just given me the best orgasm I'd ever had in my life.

"Danny'll be here in just a minute."

I felt the rumble of Hayes's words when he leaned down to whisper gruffly just above my ear. Then, he dusted a kiss on the side of my neck. It was electrifying, the sensation zipping through my body and swirling into the others. I had no idea I could *feel* this much.

My last boyfriend, a friendly, smart guy who I liked, had never even managed to bring me to orgasm. I did have a vibrator that was so good I'd occasionally wondered if it ruined me for regular sex.

"Here he is," Hayes murmured.

I simply followed where his coaxing touch on my hip led me.

Once we'd stood from the table, Hayes had reverted to being coolly polite, although he kept his touch on me the entire drive home. His palm was like a brand on my thigh as we rode through the drizzle and darkness.

He kissed me good night at the door with just a tease of his tongue before he lifted his head. "Good night, Jessica."

His eyes searched my face, and I had to clear my throat to speak. "G'night."

I was wrestling with an actual physical, magnetic pull to him. My body yearned for him, for *more*.

After a moment had stretched, Hayes asked, "Are you free next Friday?"

My head bobbed up and down in an instant, and it took me two tries to respond verbally. "Yes," I finally said, too breathlessly for my comfort.

"Perfect. Can I pick you up a little earlier, say six?"

"Yes," I managed again.

Apparently, mind-bending orgasms left me capable of nothing more than one-word sentences.

He dipped his head once more, this time brushing a chaste kiss across my lips. Except that wasn't what I wanted. After murmuring something incoherent, I reached up and slid my hand around his neck to pull him closer.

Hayes, because he was awesome, sexy, and kissed like a dream, didn't hesitate. He fit his mouth over mine and swept his tongue inside. My knees went weak again, and I was clutching his shoulders for balance when he broke free with a startled laugh.

"Next Friday," he said before stepping back.

I was frozen where I was, and he slid a hand in his pocket. "I'm waiting until you go in," he added.

My belly did a little flip, but I reached for the door handle and walked inside. The door clicked shut behind me, and I leaned against it, listening to the sound of his footsteps crossing my porch and descending the stairs.

My legs were still feeling wobbly as I pushed away from the door. My purse slid off my shoulder, falling to the floor with a soft thud. I draped my jacket over the back of the couch and kicked my shoes off as I made my way into the bathroom. Leaning my hands on the counter, I stared at myself in the mirror. My lips were puffy, my cheeks flushed, and my eyes wide.

Hayes had done what I thought was impossible. He made me lose myself with abandon. With a mental shake, I peeled off my clothes and climbed into the shower. Just thinking about how I had an orgasm in the middle of a restaurant got me hot and bothered all over again.

Chapter Ten

JESSICA

"Friday?" Sarah asked, her eyes wide.

"Yes, Friday. What's wrong with that?"

"Is that the only day of the week he goes out?"

"How am I supposed to know?" I lifted my hands in exasperation. "I've only had one dinner date with him."

"I know, and I'm still waiting for you to fill me in. How did it go?"

Sitting in one of the conference rooms at the office, we were going over the resumes and our notes from the round of interviews we had finished this morning. One thing I'd learned while running my own company was not to drag out the hiring process. Most people were looking for work because they needed a job, so if you delayed too long, someone else would snap them up. I never rushed, but once we got to the stage of interviews, I tried to make prompt decisions.

Sarah leaned back in her chair, spinning a pencil between her fingers as she eyed me. My cheeks got hot.

"Well, then," she said with a satisfied smile. "I'd say it went quite well. I don't expect you to give me all the details because you're too private for that. Please tell me he was better in bed than your college boyfriend."

My face had to be three shades of red by this point. "It wasn't like that," I insisted. "We didn't even spend the night together." Okay, so I left out the fact Hayes gave me an earth-shattering orgasm in a café, but I wasn't ready to share that.

Sarah laughed. "Well, whatever happened, it's making you all hot and bothered. I am on team Hayes. I've never even heard anything bad about the guy."

"He has his grandmother's cat. His cat is named Winston too," I offered.

"Clearly, you're meant to be then. You both have cats named Winston."

I giggled and couldn't even believe I was giggling about anything. Hayes had me feeling like a foolish girl.

There was a sharp knock, and our receptionist, Ellen, poked her head around the door. "You have a delivery."

"Me?" I pointed at my chest, honestly confused because I wasn't expecting anything.

Ellen smiled. "Yes, you."

Sarah was hot on my heels as I walked down the hallway. A massive bouquet of wildflowers was sitting on the counter surrounding Ellen's desk.

"This is for me?" I gestured to the flowers as Sarah and Ellen appeared at the end of the hallway behind me.

"Yes," Ellen said.

Sarah squealed. "Open the card," she demanded, pointing at it.

With my heart pounding and butterflies spinning in my belly, I reached for the card tucked in the flowers.

These made me think of you.
Hayes

· · ·

"Please let me see," Sarah said, holding her hands behind her back. I knew she was resisting the urge to snatch the card from me, so I handed it over.

Ellen stepped to her side, and they read the single sentence together.

Ellen looked up first. "Oh, my."

"Oh, my what?"

"He likes you," Sarah declared as she handed the card back to me.

"How do you know?"

"Hayes Maddox is not exactly a romantic guy. He's all business and mostly unapproachable. Not only did he take you out to dinner, not only is he taking it slow with you, but he found the exact kind of flowers you would love. You love wildflowers. Remember in our dorm room? You had a flower box in the window every spring filled with wildflowers. You have flowers at your house too."

"You better find a way to thank him," Ellen said solemnly.

My panic must've shown on my face because Ellen reached over and lightly squeezed my shoulder. "Jessica, it'll be fine. Obviously, he likes you just the way you are."

As we walked back down the hallway, Sarah nudged me with her elbow. "Do something awesome."

"What?" I really didn't know what to do.

"Think of something that might surprise him and do it. You're creative. You'll think of it."

Chapter Eleven

HAYES

A day after I sent the bouquet of wildflowers to Jessica, there was a knock on my office door. "Come in," I called, my eyes on the spreadsheet on my screen.

Jessica had sent me a thank-you text yesterday evening. I was deeply regretting my choice to wait a full week before I saw her again because I craved her.

Brian walked into my office. "Here." Crossing over, he set a small box wrapped in silver paper on my desk. It had a burgundy note taped on top.

He stood on the other side of my desk, a slight glint in his gaze as he looked at me. "Are you going to open it?" he finally asked.

"Are you going to insist on watching?" I countered.

"You bet."

I shifted my shoulders, rolling my neck from side to side to ease the tension starting to bundle there. It wasn't bad tension. It was anticipatory tension. I sensed this little delivery was from Jessica, and my uncommon excitement about it was unsettling.

Reaching for it, I flipped open a note on top. *To Hayes* was all it said.

I quickly unwrapped the small box. Lifting the lid, I found two things. First, a set of silver cuff links. When I turned them to the side, I smiled at the bold H carved into the surface. The other was a small piece of card stock. Lifting it, I smiled as I read it. It was a series of numbers and letters with a link.

"What the hell is that?" Brian asked.

"It's a beta code."

Brian let out a little sigh. "This is why Jessica is going to be perfect for you. Only a woman like her would get that you're probably going to masturbate over getting this beta code for one of her games in development."

I didn't care what he thought, or that he might've been right.

"Can I see the cuff links?" Brian asked. I handed them over, and he held them in his palm as he inspected them. "Very nice. They suit you."

They *were* very nice. But the beta code? I loved it.

After Brian departed, I opened up my email, pulling up the private address I'd created solely to communicate with Jessica.

Hayes: *How lucky am I to get this beta code? By the way, the cuff links are perfect.*

Friday is only three days away.

Jessica's reply came only minutes later. I loved that she wasn't coy and didn't try to drag things out.

Jessica: *You're the only person who has that beta code. Let me know what you think.*

Now, it's only 2 days, 23 hours, and 48 many minutes until Friday.

———

By the time Friday rolled around, I was doubting my ability to keep my cool when I finally saw Jessica. For starters, we had a back and forth text and email exchange about her game. I loved her brain. I wanted to climb inside and take a walk around. She was brilliant and savvy and so fucking creative.

As much as I wanted to steal her back, I knew running her own company was what gave her this freedom. I would happily partner with her on any projects she wanted.

When Danny pulled to the curb in front of her house, he glanced over his shoulder at me. He eyed me speculatively for a moment until I arched a brow in question. "I like Jessica," he offered.

"I do too. Care to share why you felt the need to let me know that?"

Danny was quiet, and his gaze considering. After a beat, he lifted his shoulder in a shrug, almost as if thinking to himself. "She deserves a good man. I know you're a good man, but sometimes you forget that."

"Are you worried I'm going to hurt Jessica?" I kept my tone light, but my heart thumped unsteadily in my chest.

Few people knew me as well as Danny did. He'd known me since I was a boy. My parents weren't wealthy, but he'd done yard work for them for years after my father messed up his shoulder. Now, I paid someone else to do yard work because Danny was too old. He wanted to work, so I had a driver solely because I wanted to give him employment.

Danny shook his head. "Oh, no. I trust

Jessica can take care of herself. But I think you really like her, and if you don't give yourself a chance for something good, you would hurt her and yourself."

I didn't even know what to say. After another silence, Danny said, "Now, go get that pretty girl and take her to a nice dinner."

As I climbed out of the car, my senses felt fully attuned. I heard a soft breeze rustling the leaves in the trees. My eyes landed on the flower boxes in the windows of Jessica's small house. I hadn't even consciously noticed them the last time I was here, but then perhaps my subconscious did. In the silvery evening light, I could see an explosion of wild, messy flowers much like the bouquet I'd sent her.

When I stood in front of her door, I realized for the first time since I'd gotten in the car tonight that I was nervous. Because I liked Jessica. I *really* liked her. Maybe it all started because of my physical attraction to her. She *was* hot, but now she was so much more.

I didn't realize I was holding my breath until the doorknob turned, and she opened the door. Her hair was down in a glossy swirl around her shoulders. I thought I spied a streak of pink mingling with the burgundy in her locks.

Her teeth dented her bottom lip as a smile unfurled across her face. "Come in." Opening the door wider, she gestured me inside. "Winston will want to say hello."

"He will?" I replied with a chuckle. As if to prove her point, Winston approached, purring up a storm as he circled my calves.

The little skirts Jessica wore were going to kill me. She had great legs, long and lithe. Once again, when she leaned over to pick up her purse, I was thinking I could just cross the room and pull that skirt up.

As if he was aware of the direction my thoughts took, Winston purred again, bumping his head against the front of my shin. "Hey, Winston," I said as I leaned down to scratch under his chin.

As I straightened, my eyes landed on the desk in the corner. Her home was warm and inviting. With glossy hardwood floors and throw rugs here and there, she had a big comfortable-looking sectional and a television mounted above the fireplace. In the corner, there were two desks situated with several computer monitors on top, all of them on at the moment.

Before I realized it, I was crossing over to

see what she was working on. I scanned, seeing the beta game I'd been playing on one of the screens. "Are you making more changes?"

"Until a game is out the door, I'm always making changes."

Jessica came to stand beside me where I had my hand leaning on her desk. One computer screen had the code she was working on with another showing the graphics. "I'm struggling with setting the difficulty," she explained. "I tend to overthink that."

We were supposed to go to dinner, but I forgot all about it.

It was a full two hours before I even noticed the time. That was with a clock in front of me the entire time on the computer monitors. We were sitting at her desk, alternating between screens as we toyed with adjusting various settings in the game. Jessica showed me some changes she had already implemented based on my feedback about the beta version she had sent over.

We were completely engrossed in work, although I didn't even think of it as work. I loved analyzing mechanisms in technology. I also loved listening to Jessica.

She was brilliant, thoughtful, creative, and so thorough. She considered every angle of every change she made. It was a major turn-on.

"Did you still want to go to dinner?" I belatedly asked.

I occupied a low stool Jessica had pulled over while she sat on her desk chair. Her hands froze on the keyboard, and she spun to face me as they dropped away. Her cheeks turned a pretty shade of pink, and I wanted to kiss her.

I'd had enough foresight to text Danny and let him know we would be leaving later because I was doing some work with Jessica. I'd told him to go home for the night because I didn't want him waiting around indefinitely. Good thing I had because I'd lost all sense of time.

"I forgot about dinner," Jessica said, catching her bottom lip in her teeth and worrying it a little.

"We missed our reservation."

Her eyes widened. She whipped her head to the side, glancing at the computer screen. When her eyes met mine again, she cast me a sheepish smile. "It's been two hours. I'm really sorry. I can get kind of absorbed."

"Same here. You weren't the only one who lost track of time."

As we stared at each other, the air around

us begin to feel heavy with a subtle hum of electricity. The hairs on the back of my neck rose in awareness. I had meant for tonight to actually be a seduction. It was supposed to be planned.

Yet here I was, apparently so enthralled with the way Jessica's brain worked that I forgot everything else. I felt the swell of my cock when I saw her slide her palms over her thighs, almost nervously. Leaning forward, I reached for her hands.

"Come here," I murmured.

Jessica stood from her chair, and she was immediately right in front of me, standing between my knees. With me seated, our faces were almost level. Her eyes searched my face, and I wanted to kiss her. So very, *very* much.

"Hayes..." she began, the frayed sound of my name in her voice like metal striking pavement and sending sparks flying high into the air.

I didn't know who leaned closer first, but inside of a millisecond, we were diving into a hot, wet kiss. My hand was sliding down her back to cup her sweet ass while the other tangled in her hair as I angled my head to the side and dove into the warm sweetness of her mouth.

She let out a little whimper when I drew

her even closer between my knees, and the thick length of my arousal brushed at the apex of her thighs. That little sound was like lightning sizzling through my body.

Our kiss was carnal, a wild tangle of lips and tongues. I craved her. It was as if I were in a desert and parched of thirst. She was water, and I couldn't get enough of her fast enough. I wanted her over me, under me, and everywhere.

I didn't even realize I was tugging at her blouse until I heard a button strike the hardwood floor. I finally lifted my head from where I'd been kissing her neck. She tasted so good, and I loved the little sounds she made at the back of her throat.

Dragging my eyes open took an effort. I sucked in a breath of air. Her gaze was half-lidded, and her lips were swollen from our kiss. Her blouse hung open, and I could see her nipples, pebbled and pressing against the thin cotton of her camisole.

I scrambled for purchase in my body, clinging to the frayed threads of my control as I stared at her. "Do you still want to go to dinner?" I asked, quite reluctantly. Because if she said yes, I would find a place to take her and save this for later, but I wanted her, and I wanted her *now*.

She was quiet for a moment, and I could hear the rush of blood in my ears with every heartbeat. She had a dazed look in her eyes, and I was relieved I wasn't the only one half out of my mind with need.

"I want you more than I want dinner."

Her words had my head dropping and my forehead falling to the sweet curve of her neck. Of course, touching Jessica sent heat racing through me. I was nibbling on that sweet skin and tracing my tongue along her collarbone when something bumped into my calves.

Jessica giggled. "Winston would like our attention."

Lifting my head, I glanced down at Winston. He was rubbing against my legs and purring. Before I could ask where her bedroom was, Jessica caught one of my hands in hers and led me into the room. I dimly took in the space. She had a tall four-poster bed with a fluffy quilt on it and tons of pillows. Perfect.

In another second, we were kissing, and I found it gratifying when she tugged as frantically at my clothes as I did at hers. I was so hard, I was practically in pain, but I didn't want to race through this. I didn't want to miss a single second of making her fly apart in my arms.

I was teasing my thumb back and forth over one of her tight nipples after she was down to nothing other than her bra and panties. I could feel her nails scoring my back as she arched into me. My knees almost gave out when she reached between us and boldly stroked her hand over my cock.

Dragging my eyes open, I drew back from her sinfully sexy mouth. I lightly pinched her nipple, and satisfaction sizzled through me when she let out a ragged moan. I needed more. *Now*. Turning, I held her close as I took the few steps until we reached the foot of her bed.

"Sit," I murmured.

Jessica's eyes lifted, her gaze sultry. "Okay." Her breathy whisper sent electricity jolting through me.

I eased her hips on the bed. All I had left on were my jeans, which she'd already un-buttoned.

"You're wearing too many clothes," she whispered, reaching toward me.

Chapter Twelve

JESSICA

Hayes captured both of my hands in his when I reached to push his jeans down. "Not yet."

His raspy voice held an edge of command to it. God, this man turned me into a puddle of need. Fortunately, I was already sitting on my bed or my knees certainly would have given out. Lacing his fingers between mine, he rested our joined hands beside my hips on the bed.

The mattress dipped slightly with his weight as he shifted closer and dropped hot kisses along my neck. Every place his lips touched felt like flames licking across the surface of my skin. My breath was coming in shallow pants, and my entire body was trembling. I felt caught in a net of sparks that sent sensation in wild spins through my body.

I cried out when his mouth closed over a nipple, shivering as his teeth scraped when he bit down lightly. In another moment, he released one of my hands and flicked my bra open where it slid down my arms to rest against the mattress.

Hayes was already moving on, his palm coasting over my belly and then dipping between my thighs. I shifted, restless to relieve the throb there. I felt as if I were already teetering on the edge of release.

I'd been turned on since I opened my door and laid eyes on him tonight. We'd worked. Of all things. Working together felt like foreplay. Now, after kisses and kisses and more kisses and having his hands on me, I just needed relief.

I was used to my mind wandering during sex. Now, all I could think about was how impatient I was to have him inside me.

"Hayes, please, I need—"

Whatever I meant to say broke with a gasping moan when he shoved my panties to the side. The blunt tip of his finger was at my entrance, circling in my slick arousal. I whimpered, and he sank two fingers inside, knuckle deep.

My hips bucked toward him. I was bereft when he withdrew, then moved away. My eyes flew open wide in dismay.

"I promise it'll be worth it," he answered my unspoken protest. He hooked his fingers over the edge of my panties, murmuring, "Lift your hips."

Hayes could've ordered me to do anything at this point. Without hesitation, I lifted my hips and shimmied them as he dragged my panties off and tossed them to the floor.

A second later, I felt his palms sliding up the insides of my calves, pausing when he kneeled on the floor before me. When his eyes lifted, the hot and intense look he gave me caused me to quiver all over.

His eyes fell again just as his hands reached the juncture at the top of my thighs. He pushed them farther apart, and his fingers trailed in my folds. "You're so hot. You make me crazy."

My pussy clenched at his words, and I shifted my hips restlessly. "So wet," he murmured as he lowered his head and blew on my sex. That subtle gust of air over my clit elicited a ragged whimper.

"Hayes." His name came out in a broken moan.

My next cry was sharp when he brought his mouth to me, dragging his tongue through my cleft in a long, lazy lick. My fists gripped the comforter as he settled in to tease me beyond coherence.

His tongue and fingers were magic. I had no idea how much time passed before I heard myself begging him again. In response, he swirled his tongue around my clit, then gave it subtle suction as he buried his fingers in me. I came in a noisy burst as pleasure ricocheted everywhere in my body.

In my sated daze, I felt him rise and heard the rustle of his jeans. When I dragged my eyes open, he was smoothing a condom on. He moved fluidly, lifting me farther back on the bed, then I felt his knees coming between my thighs. He rolled over, and I was sitting astride him. He leaned back against the headboard as he caught one of my nipples with his teeth, and I shivered all over. I was so sensitive.

I settled my weight over him, savoring the hot, thick length of him nestled against my core.

"Look at me, Jessica."

Opening my eyes, I found his dark eyes waiting, his gaze intent. Just the look had me throbbing, and it had been mere minutes since I had an intense orgasm. I felt as if we were caught in an erotic haze.

His fingers sank into my flesh as he gripped me by the hips, lifting me and guiding me down over him. The feel of him filling me was so intense I could hardly bear it. My forehead fell against his shoulder as I took shuddering breaths.

He was thick and full, creating a slight burn because it had been a while for me. A sudden worry slammed into me. Lifting my head, I said apologetically, "I can't come like this." I didn't know why I felt the need to explain, but I didn't want to let him down, and I'd never actually succeeded at coming with a guy inside me. It just didn't work, and I wasn't good at faking things, so I wanted him to know.

Hayes's gaze went serious as he searched my face. "Don't worry." Then I felt the warm suction of his mouth on my neck while he adjusted the angle of our hips and set a rhythm.

Even though I was the one riding him, I felt at his mercy and savored the surrender.

There were slow, subtle nudges deeper into my core. I was so slippery wet, the friction over my clit had me chasing for release again and thinking it had to be impossible.

It wasn't. "Come for me, Jessica. *Now*."

Chapter Thirteen

HAYES

Jessica's eyes widened in surprise just as I felt her channel convulse around me. I waited, watching as her eyes fell closed while she trembled all over. Finally, I let myself go, gripping her as my release tightened in my balls and then sizzled up my spine. I came with a rough cry of her name.

I held Jessica against me. I needed to *feel* her—her dewy skin, the ragged heaves of her breath, and the feel of her heart beating out a staccato rhythm in tune with mine.

After a few moments, she lifted her head. It took an effort to open my eyes and look at her. We were silent for a moment, and I just absorbed her. Her dark hair was mussed, and a whimsical pink lock fell forward on her cheek.

She was flushed, and her breath still came in shallow heaves. I was buried inside her, and I didn't ever want to be anywhere else. My heart felt as if it had tripped and fallen inside my chest. I thought Jessica was hot, unbearably sexy with a brainy twist I'd never known could turn my crank this hard. She was all of that, but so much more. I was pretty sure I was in over my head, solely due to my own overconfidence and miscalculation.

I had intended to blow her mind while fulfilling my hottest sexual fantasy. Doing the brilliant intern had been hands-off until now. Jessica had done what I thought impossible. She shimmered like slivers of sunshine along the edges of shades and windows of long darkened rooms in the abandoned home of my heart. The sun kept pressing through until light reclaimed the space in my heart.

My heart kept on beating as I gradually caught my breath. I didn't know what to say. In lieu of words, I looked at her hair, catching a pretty lock of pink and spinning it around my forefinger. "You added pink this week."

Jessica nodded. "Uh-huh."

Just then, the door to her bedroom popped open, and I gave her a puzzled look. She smiled sheepishly. "Winston knows how to open the door. It's an older house, and the latch isn't great, so if he pushes hard enough, it opens."

I couldn't help but chuckle. "I feel like he's our chaperone."

"He probably thinks he is," Jessica said, a glint of laughter in her eyes.

Then, her stomach growled. Her eyes widened comically, and she slapped her hand over her belly between us. My head fell back against the pillows with a hearty laugh this time. "I'm starving too, and I owe you dinner."

Jessica considered me quietly. "Don't you dare make me wait until next Friday."

As soon as she spoke, her lashes fell, and I sensed she wished she hadn't said that. I nudged my knuckles under her chin. "I won't. We can have dinner tonight and tomorrow and the next night if you'd like."

Her lashes swept upward, and her eyes met mine. "That would be nice."

"Nice?" I countered.

Chapter Fourteen

JESSICA

"I don't know." I leaned forward and clicked on the keyboard to expand the view Hayes was showing me. I felt his eyes on me and glanced sideways toward him. "What?"

"You can't make it too difficult. If you do, you lose a whole segment of gamers. I think it's a better move to create tiers of difficulty. Those who want to be more challenged will move through faster, and that's fine."

He lifted another piece of pizza from the box resting on my desk by his elbow and tore off a bite. After Winston's interruption and my stomach making its hungry state well-known, we'd gotten dressed. Hayes had offered to call and get us another reservation at the restaurant where he'd planned to take me. But when he'd seen the hesitation in my eyes, he'd suggested pizza.

After a mere two dates, I was dangerously close to falling for this man. On second thought, I didn't even know if this counted as an actual date.

I looked at the screen and the spreadsheet showing the staggered levels of difficulty for the game I was working on. Catching his eyes again, I felt my lips tugging into a reluctant smile. "You're right. I know you're right. That's my biggest weakness, always wanting to start at a higher level."

"It's because you're brilliant, and you're a woman."

I started to bristle inside, but then I saw the look in his eyes. Uncertainty flickered there but also empathy. "I'm a man, so I'm not going to pretend I understand what it's like to be a woman in the world. That would be remarkably oblivious, as well as arrogant. But I do know women have to work ten times as hard to prove their worth. In the tech world, it's even worse. Totally sexist field," he muttered, sounding disgusted. "In the gaming world within the tech world, it's particularly difficult for women. Of course, you want to prove you make smart games. And, you do. You absolutely do. But you also want to broaden your customer base. You can still make it challenging with a high level of difficulty to achieve, just also make it accessible for everyone."

I took a bite from the slice of pizza I'd set on a paper plate, considering his observation as I chewed. "I knew there was a reason I wanted to do an internship at your company," I finally said with a slow smile.

"It's not because you had a crush on me and thought I was hot?" he teased.

My cheeks went pink, but I decided to be honest. "Of course, I had a crush on you. But that wasn't why I wanted the internship. I wanted a chance to work in your coding department, and I ended up learning a lot. You're also known for not being a total asshat."

His eyes searched mine for a moment before he bit his lip and laughed. "That's high praise. I'm not an asshat."

"Toward women," I elaborated. "I did kind of think you were cold, though, and totally cocky. I still can't believe I'm sitting here with you."

This entire night had blown all my expectations into smithereens. Hayes had taken the map of the man I had in mind and torn it to pieces. Now, I was trying to put it back together and understand him. I was also trying to grasp the fierce need that beat with its own heart between us, and the raw tenderness and carnal eroticism with which he touched me.

Hayes took another bite of his pizza, and we ate quietly. I was surprised at how comfortable it was to be with him. I just wished I didn't feel so insecure, so uncertain and floundering in relationships. I mean, my God, the only reason I was sitting here with him tonight was because we had a chance encounter. I was certainly out of my depth.

I turned to look back at the computer screen, idly running calculations in my brain when I felt Hayes's palm curl on my shoulder and slide down my arm. His fingers tangled with mine when I looked his way.

"I'd never use the word crush to describe the way I felt about anyone, but you can bet I knew exactly who you were and never forgot your name. The only reason I didn't make a move on you before was because you were an intern. I even have policies about that in HR at my company," he said with a wondering laugh.

"You mean you don't chase after all the hot interns? I'm pretty sure I wasn't one of them."

The look he gave me sent licks of fire over the surface of my skin. "Jessica, hot doesn't even come close to doing you justice."

Our self-appointed chaperone, Winston, leaped onto the desk then. Hayes was lightning fast and closed the pizza box before Winston climbed in and helped himself.

"Do you need to check on your Winston?" I asked as my eyes flicked to the clock on the computer screen. I didn't even know how, but it was approaching midnight. Hayes seemed to have magical powers, and I lost all sense of time with him.

"I already texted Danny. He checked on Winston for me." For just a second, I thought I saw uncertainty flicker in his eyes. The moment passed.

He brought his eyes back to the screen, and we lost ourselves in technical talk and debating the various merits of different games.

Chapter Fifteen

HAYES

Seven weeks later

"Oh, it's on!" Jessica arched a dark brow. "You think you can beat me? You are so wrong." She gave me a saucy smile from across the room.

It was Friday night, and we'd both had long days at work. We'd fallen into a pattern of spending every weekend together. Both of us had pretty relentless and busy work schedules, so getting together during the week was hit or miss. It was on the tip of my tongue every Monday morning to ask her to just move in with me, but a tiny corner of my heart and my mind hesitated.

I knew I was in love with Jessica. But I found myself wondering if maybe she didn't return my feelings with the same intensity. As she crossed the room, my body hummed with tension. She was so fucking gorgeous. She was wearing a pair of boy shorts that hugged her curvy bottom and a loose tank top. I'd already stripped her bare and assuaged the fierce need I'd been holding at bay all week.

We'd eaten dinner and were busy bouncing between work projects. Aside from the sex, which was incredible and mind-blowing, working on projects together was the best part about hanging out with her. Business was never boring, and she got just as bogged down in the nitty-gritty of computer coding as I did.

I patted the couch beside me. "We'll see who's better. When I was a kid, I played this game with my friends all the time."

Jessica plopped down on the couch beside me, hooking a foot under her knee and taking the controller I handed to her.

Within minutes, the basketball game was a dead heat. At one point, she distracted me when I felt the silky skin of her thigh press against mine as she deftly blocked me from scoring. She let out a laugh, raising her fist in the air when she won that game.

"We're tied now, right?" Her cheeks were pink, and her eyes wide with excitement when she glanced my way. My heart tripped and fell again.

"Oh, yeah. It's tied. Another round."

When Jessica moved again, I decided I would take control of my distraction problem. "Let's change the rules."

She turned and looked at me. "What do you mean?"

"Can you play sitting here?" I patted the couch between my knees.

It felt as if sparks flew between us as her liquid brown eyes held mine. "That might not be an advantage for you," she teased.

"We'll have to see, won't we?"

With a grin, she rose, sliding her hips between my knees. My cock nestled just against the curve of her bottom, and she gave a little wiggle, purely to torture me.

"Don't forget," I murmured in her ear, "I'll get you back." I nipped her earlobe and trailed my fingertips down the side of her neck, loving how her skin pebbled under my touch.

I had no idea how much time passed, but we both sucked at the game after that. I had my fingers in her slick pussy as she rocked back against my arousal. When I drew a circle around her clit before delving into her channel, she threw her controller to the floor. "I forfeit."

Before I could even react, she had turned around and pulled down my shorts. In a hot second, the warm suction of her mouth drew me in, and I tangled my hand in her hair.

———

"No, really, I think we should try again," I insisted. "We can make it a real thing, like a tournament."

We were in my bed with my Winston purring away at the foot of it. Jessica's skin was dewy against mine where she rested on my chest. She laughed. "Oh, my God, you're too perfect."

That, that right there, made something crazy happen in my brain. Jessica was perfect, and I didn't want to play this cool anymore.

She curled her hand into a fist, resting her chin on it on my chest. "Why so serious all of a sudden?"

For a few seconds, I thought about playing it off, but I didn't. I smoothed my hand over her hair, my palm coming to rest between her shoulder blades where I sifted my fingers through her silky locks. "We're pretty perfect together."

Her eyes widened. "Yeah?"

"Don't you think? Here's the thing, Jessica. When this all started, I didn't know where it would go. It's turned into more than I expected. I don't think it's just me. I'd like to make, well, I guess to make it official that we're exclusive."

Her brow knitted as she regarded me. "I'm not the kind of girl who would date more than one person at a time anyway."

"I'm not the kind of guy who usually dates," I said, offering more honesty than I should.

Jessica was still looking at me, and the silence felt loaded. "Hayes, what do you want?"

Puzzled, I lifted my brows in question.

"With life, with relationships," she clarified.

"I don't know," I finally said. "Well, except for work."

Anxiety pricked my thoughts. I was facing up to the feelings I had for her, but I sensed she was asking for more definition. Seeing as I didn't know how to find it in my own mind, I wasn't sure what else to say.

"You *are* all business, after all," she said,

her lips kicking up in a smile that didn't quite reach her eyes. "Speaking of business, are you going to the tech and arts fundraiser next week?" Her tone was light, and the tense lines on her face softened.

"I was planning on it. Why don't we go together?"

Her brow knitted with worry, and she sat up, curling her feet under her knees. I instantly wanted to tug her back to me. "I don't know. I don't want people to get the wrong idea."

"That's something you worry about?" I pressed.

"Of course." She smoothed her hand over her hair, her eyes flashing with frustration. "For a man who understands how hard it is for women to be respected in our field, I can't believe you hadn't considered that."

"Of course, I have. But—"

She shook her head. "You know how people talk. It wouldn't surprise me if people thought I was trying to get ahead by sleeping with you." She leaned her elbows on her knees, resting her face in her hands. After a moment, she straightened, brushing her hair back. "I don't know."

"We're not just sleeping together. This isn't just some hot fling for me," I said, surprised at the fierce emotion that crested inside me.

Jessica stared at me quietly, all the while my heart felt as if it were stumbling and falling again and again.

"What are we, Hayes?"

"What do you mean?" Sarah asked.

"I don't know. It just feels like, well, he wants to commit to dating forever."

"You *are* dating." Sarah looked puzzled.

"I know that." I leaned my face in my hands, and my breath sifted through my fingers as I released a sigh. "I think I'm falling in love with him," I said when I finally lifted my head.

"Of course, you are. Hayes is totally sweeping you off your feet."

"It's not just that. But I get the sense that the words and the actual commitment are going to be hard for him."

Sarah leaned her chin on her hand as she regarded me from across the conference room table. "Maybe you're going to have to let him know how important commitment is to you. Actions are more important than words, though. Not to state the obvious."

"I know that." I paused, considering how things felt with Hayes recently. "It feels like there's a little distance between us lately. Plus, he's out of my league. It's crazy that we're together anyway."

"Why is he out of your league?" Sarah pressed, looking offended even though I'd made the observation myself. "You're smart, you're independent, and you run your own company. Very well, I might add. You don't have to push it. Maybe just give him some time."

"Fine," I grumbled. The intercom buzzed, and the day carried on. We moved through a busy afternoon and evening, and that night, I didn't see Hayes. We often didn't see each other during the workweek. My schedule was too busy, and the same was true for him.

———

"Hello, hello," a female voice said from over my shoulder.

Glancing back, I saw Mara Trent approaching. I didn't know her, but I knew of her. She was a model, and her job required her to be absolutely stunning.

Standing beside Hayes, I suddenly felt inadequate. It was hard not to feel as if I fell short with her standing right in front of us now. Mara's blond hair was pulled up in an artful twist with several strands dangling around her face. She had smoky eye shadow that illuminated her big blue eyes. She wore a strapless dress, classy and sexy.

Meanwhile, I now felt frumpy. I wore a skirt that hugged my hips and a loose silky blouse. Hayes had been talking to Harry Glenn, a CEO of another software company. He turned and cast a smile at Mara. His look was bland enough, but I didn't miss the look in her eyes. She looked practically feral.

"How are you, Mara?" he asked politely.

"Very well, Hayes. Yourself?"

"Doing well. Busy with work."

Her laughter was like soft bells. "Of course. I haven't seen you recently. Have you been to our favorite bar lately?"

Tension bundled at the base of my neck. Hayes and I teased occasionally about how our relationship had started all because of my fated bad first date at the game that I never saw. I occasionally wondered what he usually did after hours. I knew he didn't date, as he'd said as much, but I doubted he'd been a saint before seeing me.

Hayes's stance was casual and easy, but I didn't miss the subtle thread of tension in him. His eyes looked shuttered, and lines of tension bracketed his mouth. "Can't say I have. Have you met Jessica?" he asked, reaching for my hand and curling his warm palm around it.

Mara turned her gaze on me, her smile entirely polite. "I haven't had the pleasure." She held out her hand to shake. Her palm was cool, and her grip light. "You run Games in Heels? Am I right?"

"You are." I dipped my head in acknowledgment.

"I love meeting accomplished and brilliant women," Mara replied.

Uncertain what to say to that, I simply smiled.

Mara flicked Hayes another glance. "Good to see you, Hayes. Please do call."

He nodded, and Mara moved along. He dropped my hand, and his conversation continued with Harry peppering Hayes with questions about a few projects they were collaborating on. We were at the tech and arts fundraiser I'd asked Hayes about, and it was popular with the movers and shakers in the tech world.

I was the one who insisted that we not come to this function together. I was the one who insisted we interact only as we would have before. Two professionals, working in the same field and potentially collaborating on projects.

As I watched Mara sashay away—and sashay she did—I felt uncomfortable and insecure. As much as I worried about how my relationship, or whatever it was, with Hayes might be perceived, I wanted Mara to know he was with me. I wasn't just some brainy girl.

The night wore on. The experience was unusual for me. I was acutely aware of where Hayes was at all times, and I had to remind myself not to linger too much around him.

The evening was winding down, and I was departing from a conversation with Sarah and a potential supplier when I heard Mara's melodic laugh. Since when did I freaking remember another woman's laugh?

Apparently, starting tonight. When I glanced in the direction of her laughter, I saw her standing beside Hayes. He had his jacket folded over his arm. She had stepped close, and her palm was resting lightly on his forearm. I was too far away to see his face, but jealousy bolted through me, heat followed by a chill.

Frustration and embarrassment at my own reaction followed immediately on the heels of the jealousy. My eyes absorbed Hayes. He was so handsome, so hot in a suit. His suit was navy, bringing out the blue of his eyes. It was tailored, of course, and fit him delectably well.

"Jessica?" Daisy prompted from my side. She'd met me here as a favor.

Glancing at her, I asked, "What?"

"Uh, you're kind of staring. Since you told me you guys were not making your situation public, I thought you might want a reminder."

I forced my feet to move, turning my back to Hayes and Mara. "Why is he talking to her?" I muttered.

Daisy looked sympathetic enough that I felt even more ridiculous than I already did. "Maybe you shouldn't worry so much about trying to keep this private?"

I rolled my eyes. "Yeah, but you know how that might look. People would claim I was trying to find influence."

"Jessica, you are successful on your own merits. I get why you're concerned, but you can't do anything about what people might think. It's obvious Hayes really likes you, and you're making yourself crazy right now."

"How is it obvious he likes me?"

Daisy threw her hands up in the air, vaguely gesturing in the direction of him and Mara. "Every chance he gets, he's staring at you. If you're worried, he's already walked away from her."

My head whipped in that direction so fast, I could've given myself whiplash. Daisy chuckled. "Whatever you do, you need to calm down and just let this be what it is."

Looking back at her, I willed my cheeks to cool. "What do you mean?"

"I know you. This isn't a casual thing for you. As far as I can tell, it's not for Hayes either. Unless you don't plan to ever date, you might as well figure out how you're going to handle things like feelings." My friend's eyes were warm and understanding, and my heart thumped erratically.

I fiddled with the bracelet on my wrist, twisting it in circles. "I didn't plan to date anyone who was involved in the same business," I finally mumbled in reply.

Daisy gaped at me. "How are you going to meet anyone?"

"You're the one who signed me up for

that stupid dating app. That could've worked out if I hadn't been matched with an asshole," I said tartly, finally feeling like I could throw a zinger her way about my disastrous date with Chad.

My zinger went nowhere. Daisy twisted her lips and rolled her eyes. "Good thing you went on that date even if it was a disaster. You ran into Hayes because of that date."

I glared at her. Glancing at my watch, I said, "I'm going home. Shall we catch a ride together?"

"Sure. I'll grab our coats," she offered. "Why don't you go ahead and see if you can get a car outside?"

I tapped open my car service app and entered a ride. Daisy lived only a few blocks away from me with Tristan and their daughter. Moments later, I was standing on the sidewalk waiting for her, who had just texted me that she ran into a colleague from work. She said she'd be out in a few minutes.

The light drizzle was typical for Seattle on any given day and night throughout the year. I scanned the streets, looking for the red sedan with the license plate listed as our ride on the car service app. As I surveyed the area, my eyes snagged on Hayes's car. I recognized it because I'd ridden in it with some regularity over the past month or so. He was standing beside it with his hand curled around the door handle to the back seat. Freaking Mara was there. She said something to him, and then he opened the door, and she climbed inside.

I panicked, hot jealousy spinning in my stomach and making me feel a little sick. I couldn't believe he was actually taking her home. I suddenly wondered if she knew Winston. His Winston was ridiculously free with affection. Unlike my Winston, who was more reserved and needed time to get to know someone.

"Fuck, fuck, fuck." Taking a deep breath, I willfully turned away, relieved when I saw Daisy hurrying down the stairs and across the sidewalk toward me. Just then, my eyes landed on the red sedan pulling up in front of the pick-up area. With a quick scan of the license plate, I knew our ride was here.

We got in the car, and Daisy was blessedly distracted. If she noticed I was out of it and barely paying attention to her, she didn't comment on it. I was relieved because I was too embarrassed to tell her that the man who she thought really liked me was taking another woman home tonight.

"I have a good feeling about you and

Hayes," she said, flashing me a smile as she slipped her phone into her purse a few minutes later.

"Yeah?"

She gave me a confident smile. "I do. Have a little faith."

I managed a nod, but I didn't have much faith when it came to relationships. I'd never even had a casual relationship that involved sex. I had my high school boyfriend, my college boyfriend, and then nothing until my one date with Chad, and now Hayes. Just thinking about the sight of Mara's glossy blond hair glinting under the streetlights when she leaned over before getting in the car sent my stomach into a sick turn.

Chapter Seventeen

HAYES

"Oh, come on, Hayes. Just for a little fun," Mara practically purred.

"I offered you a ride, Mara. Nothing more."

She actually pouted and let out a little calculated huff. Even that, I surmised, was intended to sound sexy.

Mara was beautiful. She just didn't attract me anymore. She'd been a relationship of convenience, though I don't know if I would even go so far as to call it a relationship. More of an occasional arrangement.

Tonight, I'd been feeling out of sorts the entire evening. I was trying to respect Jessica's request that we not make our relationship public, yet it was driving me nuts. I was also frustrated with myself because trying to keep my distance from her only illuminated how much she meant to me.

Mara couldn't know it, and I obviously wouldn't tell her because it would hurt her feelings, but her showing up had highlighted how much I wanted Jessica.

Once upon a time, someone like Mara was all I wanted. She was sexy, there were no complications, and she was willing to push boundaries. And yet, now that held no allure for me. No woman had ever turned me on the way Jessica did.

Everything with Jessica was for *us*. Together. My feelings transcended desire. With Mara, there was no emotion twined within desire. I craved the emotion now, the intimacy and intensity of it. I could only find that with Jessica.

When Danny pulled up in front of Mara's condominium building, she smiled over at me. "Are you sure?" she asked.

When her tongue darted out and dragged across her bottom lip, I knew it was calibrated and all for show. She couldn't know that only deflated me even more. I'd had a taste of Jessica—raw, unvarnished, and entirely authentic. She was so refreshing, and I missed her.

"I'm sure, Mara."

She gave me a considering look. "Are you dating someone? I can't help but be nosy."

I held her gaze evenly. "My private life is private." Turning, I tapped the button to unlock the doors. Danny knew his cue. He was out and opening Mara's door within seconds.

After she disappeared with a dash through the rain into her condominium building, Danny looked over his shoulder at me. "Where is Miss Jessica?"

His tone was conversational and low-key, but I sensed a hint of reproach in it. "Not with me," I said pointedly. "But not by my choice."

Danny turned away and smoothly pulled off the curb a moment later. "If it was by her choice, did you try to persuade her otherwise? She's a smart girl, so she's going to need persuading."

"Are you implying I'm not a good bet for her?" I asked, feeling a little defensive even though I was trying to tease.

"Not exactly. However, you do have a reputation. It's for being a ruthless businessman, and dating beautiful women with whom you never get serious. I don't even know if you can count what you do as dating. Jessica will expect more, and she deserves more."

I lifted my hands, dropping them with a thwack on the car seat. "She doesn't want us to be public. She's concerned about how it might look for her as a woman. I don't agree. I understand her point, which is why I'm respecting it, but she means more than that to me. I tried to tell her that once it was clear what we had was genuine, any rumors would pass."

"Did you tell her you loved her?"

Danny might as well have punched me in the chest. Once again, my heart felt as if it had tripped and fallen. At my silence, he added, "Bet you didn't."

"Danny, how's that going to make a difference? She doesn't want us to be public."

"If you love her, you tell her and figure the rest out later."

I wanted to argue, but I felt a little sick about it. I *did* love Jessica, and I had to face the reality that I was being a coward about it.

"Danny—" I began.

He cut me off. "I wouldn't be so direct, Hayes, if I didn't think I was right. Your parents loved each other very much, and they adored you. When your mama died, it nearly killed your father, and I know that's why you're afraid. Do you think he would trade what he had with her?"

My heart ached a little bit, and I took a deep breath. "No," I reluctantly replied. My parents had had a genuine marriage of love. When my mother died after a brief battle with ovarian cancer, my father had been despondent. Yet, I knew he'd do it all over again even if he knew how it would end.

When I got home, I immediately texted Jessica. "Winston misses you. Does your Winston miss me?"

She didn't reply, and I fretted. I wasn't one to fret, so that pissed me off.

Chapter Eighteen

JESSICA

Three days passed, and I was irritable and heartsick and jealous. Hayes had texted me, and I'd ignored him that night. When I woke, I replied, telling him that I'd already been asleep. I'd been holding him at bay since then.

My phone chimed again. I spun my phone around on my desk to see another text from Hayes. *I'm starting to think you're avoiding me. Did something happen?*

"Yes, I'm avoiding you, dumbass," I muttered aloud at my phone. "How can you not know what happened? You took Mara home. I have eyes."

I'd been pummeled with doubts and insecurity over the past few days. To manage the warring factions of doubts arguing in my brain, I'd thrown myself into work with relentless focus. It was a huge problem that I had given Hayes my current project in beta. To keep it on track for production, I had to finalize all the changes we'd made. Every single one had me thinking of him.

My phone chimed again. *Jessica, I know when I'm being ignored. I might do something stupid if you won't at least talk to me.*

I pushed my phone away. On second thought, I snatched it back and opened his text, replying with a single name. *Mara.*

There was no immediate reply. Although it made me feel even more heartsick, his silence reinforced what I thought had happened. Hours later, Ellen poked her head into my office. "You have an unexpected visitor."

"I'm busy," I replied. That wasn't entirely true, but I just wasn't in the mood to see anyone.

"It's Mara Trent."

"What?" I finally looked up from what I'd been working on.

"She says it's really important."

My curiosity got the better of me. "Send her back. If I tap the intercom button while she's in here, please come rescue me."

Ellen grinned and nodded before leaving

my office. A moment later, Ellen opened the door again. "Her office is right here," Ellen said in a cheery voice.

Mara stepped through the door, looking straight out of a magazine. Dressed demurely in a dove gray blazer, she wore a fitted navy top underneath and matching pants. Even though everything she wore was perfectly appropriate, she somehow made it all sexy.

Meanwhile, I sat there with my hair up in a messy ponytail, a skirt I'd thrown on quickly this morning, and a denim jacket over a fitted T-shirt. If I'd needed a reminder of what I wasn't, I guess I had it.

The door clicked shut behind Mara, and I stood, gesturing to the chair across from my desk. "Please have a seat."

I sat back down when she did, and I smoothed my damp palms over my skirt, relieved she couldn't see my restless hands under my desk. "What can I do for you?" I asked, annoyed that my voice came out a little scratchy.

"I came to tell you that nothing happened with Hayes last weekend. And before you go thinking he put me up to this, he didn't. I ran into him at the coffee shop, and he looks miserable. When I asked him what was wrong, he told me I was permanently banned from ever requesting a ride home. He can be kind of an asshole." Her tone was wry.

I stared at her and choked on a laugh. The threat of tears welled in my eyes as I tried to calm the jumble of emotions racing through me. "Why are you telling me this?"

"Hayes is too proud to say anything, but I'm nosy, so I asked around. Rumor has it he's totally smitten with you. If you've cut him off because you saw him give me a ride home, I thought I should set the record straight. Not only was it just a ride but Hayes turned me down when I asked for more. Before you go thinking anything else, I wasn't secretly in love with him, nor am I pining for him. He's just a man, and he has a lot of money. I think he really likes you, and it appears maybe, just maybe, you brought him to his knees." I must've been staring agog at her because she laughed softly. "If you like him, or maybe even more, you should talk to him. You are well suited."

"You think?" My question slipped out before I could stop it, and my cheeks went hot. Not for the first time, I wished I wasn't always so easy to read.

Mara leaned forward. "Yes. Don't get me wrong, Hayes is sexy, and he's powerful, and he's all about conveying the image that he does, which is that of an untouchable businessman. But he's actually a nice guy, and I think you know that. I always figured someday he'd fall for someone. I've known him since I did some work for an advertising campaign for his company a few years ago. You're brilliant. My goodness, even I know who you are. You've won awards and all that. Maybe we don't work in the same field, but I respect a woman who's made her way in a man's world. It's not an easy thing to do."

My mouth dropped open, and I snapped it shut. "That's a part of the problem. I told Hayes I wasn't ready for us to be public because I'm concerned how it'll look for me. I was an intern at his company once."

"Did you sleep with him when you were an intern?" she asked bluntly.

"Oh, God no. He hardly even looked at me."

"Oh, I'm sure he did. You're his type with the brainy, sexy librarian vibe. I'm not you, and obviously, I'm not trying to make my way up in the computer and gaming field. But I do know that it doesn't really matter what anyone thinks in the long run. Screw them all. If you want him, go get him."

Chapter Nineteen

HAYES

What could I do to fix a non-fixable problem? The problem being I knew Jessica had a point. There would be chatter when our relationship became public. Because that was how the world treated women. It wouldn't matter that she could point to the success she'd already had establishing and running her own company. It wouldn't matter that she was brilliant in her own right. It wouldn't matter that she hadn't partnered with my company on any projects.

I couldn't resist hoping she would, though, because I fully intended to partner with her on projects going forward. She had a more creative brain than I did when it came to gaming.

It *would* matter that she'd once been an intern at my company. There would probably be speculation that we had a relationship back then. I could deny it vehemently and unequivocally, but that would only pour more fuel on the brushfire of gossip.

None of this changed the fact that I was in love with Jessica, and I missed her. I was going to do the only thing I could do. I wanted to make sure she knew how I felt.

Heading down to the market, I scouted out the wildflowers. Specifically, burgundy and pink. I was going to deliver them personally.

After I found what I wanted, I slipped the jump drive with the game I wanted Jessica's help on in the middle of the bouquet tied on a ribbon. When I reached her office building, I was surprised to see Mara leaving. A sense of dread tightened in my gut when she approached me.

"Mara..." I began.

She held a neatly manicured hand up. "Please stop. I'm glad to see you here. I hope those are for Jessica."

"Mara—" I began again, only to get her palm once more.

"I know you didn't talk to me about this. But word travels, so I took it upon myself to come tell Jessica that you turned me down last weekend and that you were just being a gentleman and giving me a ride. She's lovely, and I'm all for love."

I stared back at Mara for a moment and chuckled. "Fair enough. You are, as always, well-connected."

"I'd like credit at the wedding," she teased. "Kidding," she added when my eyes widened slightly. "Go get your girl, Hayes." Mara smiled, and I realized there was more to her than I'd considered.

On the elevator ride up to Jessica's office, I realized my plan had a major flaw. I didn't know if she was busy. Obviously, she'd made time to see Mara, but that didn't mean she didn't have something lined up the second Mara walked out the door. Well, fuck it. I was already here with the flowers, so I would wait as long as necessary.

When I pushed through the glass door into the waiting area, a receptionist looked up from a desk. A bright smile spread across her face. "Hello, how can I help you?"

"I'm hoping Jessica Slater is available."

"Do you have an appointment?" the receptionist asked.

Great, so that was how it was going to go today. "I don't. I'll wait, if necessary."

Chapter Twenty

JESSICA

"Say that again."

"Hayes Maddox would like to see you. He has a giant bouquet," Ellen repeated.

Sarah practically put burn marks on the carpet as she skidded into my office from hers across the hallway. "He has burgundy and pink flowers, and they're wildflowers," she shout-whispered.

"How do you know?"

My pulse was racing, and I felt crazy nervous with my belly spinning flips.

"Because I peeked, you dummy. I'm nosy. He's going for a big romantic gesture!" Sarah couldn't stop whispering so loudly she might as well have been using a megaphone.

I was still trying to recover from my

unannounced meeting with Mara, and now Hayes was here. Cue the panic.

Ellen and Sarah were standing in my doorway, looking at me very expectantly. "Um, tell him I'll be a few minutes," I finally said.

Ellen, because she was calm and put together, simply nodded. "I'll give you five minutes. Sound good?"

"Sure." As if five minutes would somehow help me pull my shit together.

Ellen disappeared, but Sarah didn't. She rested her hand on her hip and strolled from the doorway to stop in front of my desk. "Burgundy and pink."

"Right, I heard you the first time."

"You don't get the point of that?" She threw her hands up in the air, clearly exasperated with me.

"I don't know what you mean." I was clearly still not catching on.

"You have burgundy and pink streaks in your hair. God, you're so slow sometimes. The flowers would've been romantic all by themselves, but he actually matched them to your two favorite colors. He did that on purpose." She drummed a single fingertip on my desk in emphasis.

I stared at her blankly for a minute, and

my heart felt as if it flipped over. Taking a deep breath, I asked, "Do you really think he meant to do that?"

Sarah cocked her head to the side, shaking it slowly as she sighed. "Yes. I really think so." Her eyes bounced up to the clock on my wall. "You only have three minutes now."

"Oh, my God." My hands fluttered all over my desk. Why, I had no idea. I started randomly tidying it.

Sarah lifted her head to stare at the ceiling. "Oh, my God, she's straightening her desk."

"Is it necessary for you to narrate what I'm doing?" I muttered. I pressed my hands flat against my thighs, willing them to stop shaking.

Sarah rounded my desk, stopping beside me. "You're going to be fine. I think you should take Mara's advice."

Of course, I had immediately gone to her office and filled her in after Mara's unannounced and startling visit only a few minutes earlier. "Remind me what that was."

She pulled me into a quick and fierce hug. I clung to her as if she were a lifeboat in the ocean. She stepped back.

"You know you want him, so do something about it. I don't know exactly what she said, but that was the gist of it, right?"

I started giggling hysterically. Sarah was trying to repeat advice I'd repeated from Mara to her. "If this is the telephone game, at least we're only three steps in."

She grinned. "Exactly. I'm going back to my office because you're a big girl and you can totally handle this. You're brilliant, you're beautiful, you're a fucking CEO, and you're totally worth it."

With that, Sarah hurried out of my office. The door clicked shut behind her, and I sank into my desk chair. I felt ridiculous. My cell phone chimed on my desk.

I reflexively reached for it and spun it to face me. A banner with Hayes's name flashed on the screen. The butterflies that had taken up residence did another turn in my belly, and my pulse managed to kick up yet another notch. Sliding my shaky thumb across the screen, I opened his text.

Just checking in. I'm waiting, and there's a whole minute left. I thought I could get the hard part out of the way first. I love you.

My body felt as if I were a carbonated drink that had been shaken too hard. Joy fizzed in every cell and threatened to overflow. Lifting my phone, I managed to type out a reply.

You win. Because you got over yourself first. I love you too.

I hit send, slowly setting my phone down and trying not to drop it because my hands were still trembling. I looked up at the clock just as the minute hand finished its revolution, and Hayes came into view through my glass door.

I hurried over and swung it open. He clasped a blown glass vase in his hands with an explosion of wildflowers spilling over its edges. His gaze met mine, somber and searching and intense. Oh-so-intense.

"Did you get my text?" we asked each other, our voices crossing over.

I was nodding as he shook his head. "I think I was walking down the hallway. As soon as your receptionist let me go, I wasn't waiting. I love you," he said, repeating his text.

Throwing my arms around him, I murmured, "I love you too," squishing the gorgeous flowers between us.

Hayes managed to set the vase on the edge of my desk without letting me go. His arms folded around me, pulling me into a full-body clench.

"I kind of freaked," I mumbled into his chest. "Sorry I didn't tell you what I was thinking when I saw you give Mara a ride home."

He smoothed my hair, his voice right beside my ear where his face was tucked into my neck. "It's okay. I'm sorry too. It was just a ride, but I can imagine it didn't look good. I hope she told you I didn't put her up to coming to talk to you," he said when he finally lifted his head.

I took a deep breath because I simply needed to inhale Hayes's scent. He always smelled a little crisp, and his shirt smelled like clean laundry. Finally, I looked up at him. "She did tell me that. I'm ridiculous."

He shook his head, his eyes scanning my face before he lifted a hand to brush a wayward lock of hair off my cheek and tuck it behind my ear. Just that subtle brush of his fingertips against the sensitive skin there sent goose bumps chasing over the surface of my skin.

"You're not ridiculous. You're absolutely right about the possible rumors about us and how things might look. I can't change that because the world sucks, and it's really hard on women, especially in our field. But I still love you, and I'd rather face it with you."

My eyes stung with tears, and I had to swallow through the emotion clogging my throat.

"Same here. I'm sorry I doubted you. Mara even told me you turned her down."

Hayes leaned his head back, closing his eyes with a sigh. In another second, he leveled his gaze with mine with a look so intense, my breath seized in my lungs. "You need to understand that once I was with you, that was it for me."

Although I was crystal clear that nothing had passed between Hayes and Mara, I couldn't help but voice the tiny insecurities chasing their tails in my brain. "Just so you know, but I know I'm not your usual type and if I'm maybe not as—"

Hayes shook his head sharply as his hand slid down to cup my nape. "Jessica, what you and I have is everything I ever wanted," he murmured.

His thumb was brushing lightly along my throat, sending licks of fire across my skin. I took a breath, feeling the press of my nipples against his chest. Although I was overcome with emotion, nothing could keep my body from its instinctive response to being close to Hayes.

Since I didn't know what other words to

use, I leaned up and pressed an open-mouthed kiss right over the divot at the base of his throat. His hand tightened in my hair, and then we were kissing and kissing and kissing. Hayes's hands were traveling roughly over my body as my own greedy touch mapped his chest and clutched at him.

We were snapped out of our passionate kiss by a sharp knock on my door. "Unless you're into putting on a show," Sarah called through the glass as she walked by, "you might want to leave."

His chuckle rumbled against my ear when I tucked my face against his chest. When I peeked out from the shelter of his arms, the hallway was blessedly empty. With my office door all glass, there wasn't much privacy to be had.

"Can I steal you away?" he asked.

"Of course."

"If you're working on something, I can wait," he added.

"I don't want to wait," I said firmly. "I appreciate that you respect my work." A smile tugged at my lips as I trailed my fingertips along the stubbled edge of his jaw. "Did you forget to shave today?" I asked as he stepped back.

He cast me a sheepish grin. "I've been distracted. I missed you."

I felt a little bashful as I took a step back. Reaching over, I stroked my fingers down the side of the blown glass vase. When I looked up, I saw Hayes was looking down at his phone, his lips curving into a smile. "What do I win?" he asked when he brought his eyes to mine.

"What do you want to win?" I teased, that fizzy joy spinning through my veins.

"Just you."

We stared at each other, smiling, until I heard footsteps in the hallway again. "Sarah thinks the flowers are to match my hair," I commented as I glanced back at the bouquet of wildflowers.

"Sarah happens to be right," Hayes said as he stepped closer, sliding his arm around my waist where his palm rested possessively on my hip.

"That's kind of romantic," I murmured, feeling hot all over.

"I was trying. Did you notice the other thing?"

Puzzled, I looked back at the flowers, searching until my eyes landed on the thin silk ribbon and the jump drive tied to it. Reaching for it, I asked, "What's this?"

"My new project. I could use your help."

"Hayes, you don't need my help."

"Yeah, I do, sweetheart. I might be good at figuring out details and logistics and difficulty levels, but you're more creative. My thinking is a little dry and technical sometimes."

I opened my mouth to protest again, but he shook his head as he lifted a hand to trail his knuckles along my cheekbone. "It's true, and I don't mind admitting it. We can look at it together tonight. After dinner."

"Just dinner?"

His gruff laugh sent fire chasing over my skin.

Chapter Twenty-One

HAYES

Jessica's eyes held mine, her lips curling in a saucy smile. "I told you I would win."

I almost laughed, but my release tightened in my balls as she rose up and down, sheathing me one more time in her silky, clenching core. She cried out right when everything in me sizzled to a crescendo.

Moments later, I was still trying to catch my breath. Jessica was a warm, luscious bundle in my arms, and I was still buried deep inside her. "I could live like this," I murmured into her hair.

She lifted her head and shook it. "I don't think so."

"No?" I teased as I lightly cupped her

breast and rolled her still pebbled nipple between my thumb and forefinger, savoring her soft whimper.

"You like to use your brain too much," she said, trying to be serious.

"I might like using your body more than my brain," I mused as I let my hand slide over the soft curve of her belly and gave her generous hip a squeeze. Of course, her comment got the wheels in my brain turning. "You really think we should have two bosses?" I asked, referencing our conversation some indeterminate amount of time earlier about my latest project.

"Yes. Games last longer, and there is more gameplay and more complicated dynamics when you have two alpha bosses in them. My favorite suggestion would be to make one of them have a secret code for players to crack."

"Oh, I love that idea."

Jessica laughed and shimmied off my lap. "We have work to do." She gave me a quick grin over her shoulder as she practically pranced into my shower. I followed her and made good use of our time there.

Not much later, we were at my workstation at home where I had four monitors. We stayed up late working, and I loved it. But then, I loved every minute I spent with Jessica. The best part? When she left me breathless with another round and I got to fall asleep beside her.

EPILOGUE

Jessica Slater and Hayes Maddox unveiled their latest collaboration. They won't reveal whose idea it was, but it's the hottest game of 2024. Gamers are working feverishly to crack the code that reveals a secret boss.

Meanwhile, the tech duo continues to reign over their respective businesses. Any rumors or questions about their relationship were quashed when they had the tech society wedding of the year. The public wasn't invited to the wedding itself, however the reception party was a massive competition for gamers in Seattle.

Time and again, Hayes Maddox makes it clear Jessica Slater is the brains behind their partnership. They say love conquers all, and in their case, that seems to be true.

———

Thank you for reading Hayes & Jessica's story! Sign up for my newsletter, so you can receive information about upcoming new releases & receive a FREE copy of one of my books: http://jhcroixauthor.com/subscribe/

If you'd like more stories in Seattle, check out The Play. Liam is a British footballer who falls for Olivia, his doctor. A twist of forbidden heats up this swoon-worthy & laugh-out-loud romance. Don't miss Liam & Olivia's story.
Free on all retailers!

Up next in the Fireweed Harbor Series is One More Time.

McKenna ends up with a black eye when she meets Jack. Sort of, but not really, his fault.

Black eye aside, the earth shakes when she meets him. But McKenna only believes in love for other people. Unlucky might as well be her middle name.

Jack doesn't care about luck and he's a breath-stealing, swoony hotshot firefighter. He can't forget McKenna, although she makes him forget plenty of other things.

Don't miss McKenna & Jack's swoony, hot and intense romance!

One More Time - due out February 2024!

For more swoony romance...

This Crazy Love kicks off the Swoon Series - small town southern romance with enough heat to melt you! Jackson & Shay's story is epic - swoon-worthy & intensely emotional. Jackson just happens to be Shay's brother's best friend. He's also *seriously* easy on the eyes. Shay has a past, the kind of past she would most definitely like to forget. Past or not, Jackson is about to rock her world. Don't miss their story! Free on all retailers!

Burn For Me is a second chance romance for the ages. Sexy firefighters? Check. Rugged men? Check. Wrapped up together? Check. Brave the fire in this hot, small-town romance. Amelia & Cade were high school sweethearts & then it all fell apart. When

they cross paths again, it's epic - don't miss
Cade's story!
Free on all retailers!

For more small town romance, take a visit to
Last Frontier Lodge in Diamond Creek. A
sexy, alpha SEAL meets his match with a
brainy heroine in Take Me Home. Marley is
all brains & Gage is all brawn. Sparks fly
when their worlds collide. Don't miss Gage &
Marley's story!
Free on all retailers!

FIND MY BOOKS

Thank you for reading Just A Kiss! I hope you enjoyed the story. If so, you can help other readers find my books in a variety of ways.

1) Write a review!
2) Sign up for my newsletter, so you can receive information about upcoming new releases & receive a FREE copy of one of my books: http://jhcroixauthor.com/subscribe/
3) Like and follow my Amazon Author page at https://amazon.com/author/jhcroix
4) Follow me on Bookbub at https://www.bookbub.com/authors/j-h-croix

5) Follow me on Instagram at https://www.instagram.com/jhcroix/
6) Like my Facebook page at https://www.facebook.com/jhcroix

Fireweed Harbor Series
Make You Mine
Dare To Fall
Be The One
One More Time - due out February 2024!
Light My Fire Series
Wild With You
Hold Me Now
Only Ever Us
Fall For Me
Keep Me Close
With Every Breath
All It Takes
Take Me Now
Meant To Be
Dare With Me Series
Crash Into You
Evers & Afters
Come To Me
Back To Us
Take Me There
After We Fall

Swoon Series
This Crazy Love
Wait For Me
Break My Fall
Truly Madly Mine
Still Go Crazy
If We Dare
Steal My Heart
Into The Fire Series
Burn For Me
Slow Burn
Burn So Bad
Hot Mess
Burn So Good
Sweet Fire
Play With Fire
Melt With You
Burn For You
Crash & Burn
That Snowy Night
Brit Boys Sports Romance
The Play
Big Win
Out Of Bounds
Play Me
Naughty Wish
Diamond Creek Alaska Novels
When Love Comes
Follow Love

Love Unbroken
Love Untamed
Tumble Into Love
Christmas Nights
Last Frontier Lodge Novels
Take Me Home
Love at Last
Just This Once
Falling Fast
Stay With Me
When We Fall
Hold Me Close
Crazy For You
Just Us

ACKNOWLEDGMENTS

So much gratitude to you, my readers! Writing can be lonely and doubts can be noisy. If you are a new-to-me reader, thank you for taking a chance on this story. If you are a long-time reader, thank you for taking chance after chance on my stories.

Many thanks to my editor for helping me give Jessica and Hayes the best story, and to my proofreader, Terri D., for catching all the details. Of course, hugs to my early readers.

As always, my husband keeps me laughing and makes sure I have the time and space to write. My dogs keep me company and our morning runs together help me with plotting.

xoxo
J.H. Croix

ABOUT THE AUTHOR

USA Today Bestselling Author J. H. Croix lives in a small town with her husband and two spoiled dogs. Croix writes contemporary romance with sassy women and alpha men who aren't afraid to show some emotion. Her love for quirky small-towns and the characters that inhabit them shines through in her writing. Take a walk on the wild side of romance with her bestselling novels!

Places you can find me:
jhcroixauthor.com
jhcroix@jhcroix.com

facebook.com/jhcroix

instagram.com/jhcroix

bookbub.com/authors/j-h-croix